Songman

Also by Allan Baillie

Adrift
Little Brother
Riverman
Eagle Island
Megan's Star
Mates
Hero
The China Coin
Little Monster
The Bad Guys
Magician

Picture Books

Drac and the Gremlin
Bawshou Rescues the Sun
(with Chun-Chan Yeh)
The Boss
Rebel!

ALLAN BAILLIE

Songman

VIKING

Viking
Penguin Books Australia Ltd
487 Maroondah Highway, PO Box 257
Ringwood, Victoria 3134, Australia
Penguin Books Ltd
Harmondsworth, Middlesex, England
Viking Penguin, A Division of Penguin Books USA Inc.
375 Hudson Street, New York, New York 10014, USA
Penguin Books Canada Limited
10 Alcorn Avenue, Toronto, Ontario, Canada M4V 3B2
Penguin Books (N.Z.) Ltd
182-190 Wairau Road, Auckland 10, New Zealand

First published by Penguin Books Australia, 1994
1 3 5 7 9 10 8 6 4 2

Typeset in Raleigh by Midland Typesetters, Maryborough, Victoria
Made and printed in Australia by Australian Print Group, Maryborough, Victoria

National Library of Australia
Cataloguing-in-Publication data:

Baillie, Allan, 1943- .
Songman.

ISBN 0 670 85662 2.

I. Title.

A823.3

There are several people without whose help this book could not have been written. For giving me generous slabs of their time and expertise I wish to thank:

At Yirrkala: Nguliny Burarrwanga; Merrkiyawuy Ganambarr; the chairman of the Yirrkala Dhanbul Council, Bakamumu Marika; Steve Fox; and my Yolngu family.

Elcho Island (Galiwinku): Michael Cooke of Batchelor College, with Helen Nungalurr; Dorothy Bepuka; Jackie Ngululuwidi.
Milingibi: Jessie Murarrgirarrgi.
Warruwi: Molly Adadawa; Paul Naragoidj.
Maningrida: Noel Cooper; Jimmy Gularawuna.
Ramingining: Rose Gaykamangu.

Nhulunbuy: Annie and Mal Matthews.

Darwin: Peter Spillett of the Darwin Museum.

Sydney: National Maritime Museum; Anne Tang.

Ujung Pandang: H.H.D. Mangemba, Dr Andi Zainal Abidin Farid and Lalu Abd Khalik of Universitas '45'; Taufik.

Galesong: Mustari

Bira: Abdul Hakim; Riswan

My sources for researching the background for *Songman* include:

The Voyage to Marege by C. C. Macknight (Melbourne University Press, 1976)
A Black Civilization by Lloyd Warner (1926)
The World of the First Australians by R.M. & C.H. Berndt (Lansdowne, 1981)
Bush Food by Jennifer Isaacs (Weldon)
Sorcerers and Healing Spirits by Janice Reid (Australian National University, 1983)
Makassar and Northwest Arnhem Land: Missing Links and Living Bridges, edited by Michael Cooke (Batchelor College)
Makassar Sailing by G.E.P. Collins (Cape, 1937)
The Sojourners by Eric Rolls (University of Queensland Press, 1988)
The East Indiamen by Russell Miller (Time Life Books)
Daily Life in Rembrandt's Holland by Paul Zumthor (Weidenfeld & Nicolson, 1962)
The Dutch in the Seventeenth Century by K.H.D. Haley (Thames and Hudson, 1972)
The Dutch Seaborn Empire, 1600–1800 by C.R. Boxer (Hutchinson, 1965)

In 1720, Australia was a vast mystery to the rest of the world.

In the west and the north it had been named New Holland but navigators considered it a wasteland.

The bored and mutinous crew of a passing Dutch ship had called a stretch of the northern coast 'Arnhem' Land, after their ship.

But Arnhem Land in New Holland was also called Marege, and a part of Arnhem Land was also the Land of the Yolngu . . .

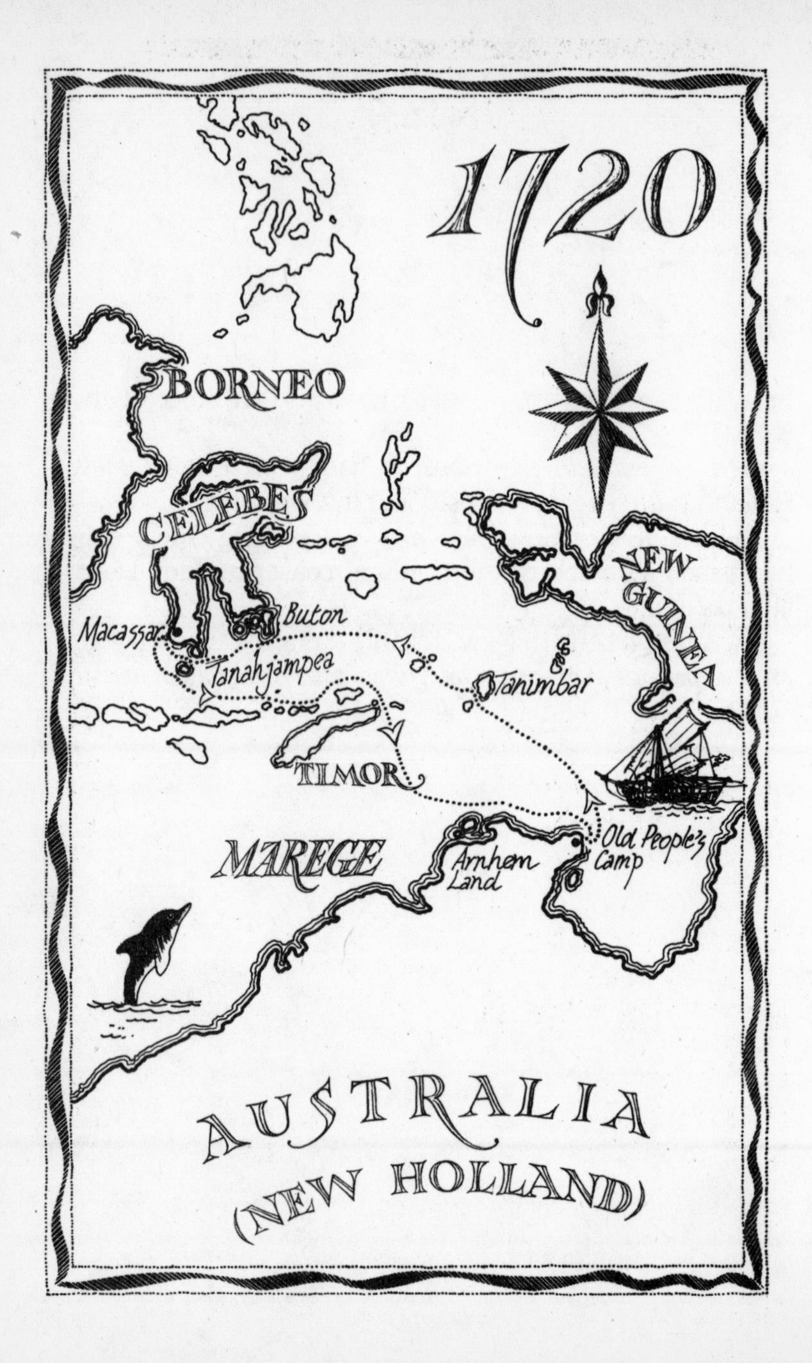
1720
BORNEO
CELEBES
Buton
Macassar
Tanahjampea
Tanimbar
NEW GUINEA
TIMOR
MAREGE
Arnhem Land
Old People's Camp
AUSTRALIA
(NEW HOLLAND)

CONTENTS

Part One

Part Two

Part Three

Part Four

Part One

1 THE SHADOW

Nhina warraw' ŋura,
ŋaku warryun malwarra
Nhama djambatjŋu
Mirrinyu.
Mayan namba
Wuŋuli

Sitting down in the shade,
Pulling the canoe into the water
Looking for dugong.
Clouds standing in the sea
The shadow stays with them ...

(Songman, Rraywala)

At first the shadow seemed a trick of light in the water.

Yukuwa thought he saw a movement in the black deep before he thrust his paddle into the sea.

He wrinkled his nose. *Thought* you saw something. Nothing's there. Maybe shifting sand, drifting weed. You don't see things. It is only Dawu who sees things.

'Come on, boy. You're paddling like a crab.' And that was Dawu, sounding like a treeful of wasps. He'd been like that for a moon.

Yukuwa forgot the shadow he didn't see and drove

the canoe towards the last glow of the sun. The sea was darkening as an angry mass of cloud rolled across the sky. 'Maybe a storm,' he said.

Dawu squinted back at him, his beard catching the breeze. 'Leave the Lightning Serpents to me, boy.'

Yukuwa glared under his eyebrows. Yes, Teacher Dawu, whatever you say. But what if a Lightning Serpent scorches your beard? What if this wobbly bark canoe falls apart in the waves?

He watched the light flickering in the clouds.

Just a moment. This canoe is not wobbly and it doesn't fall apart in the waves. It has been made by an expert. Definitely.

Yukuwa let the canoe roll a little as he leaned on his paddle.

'Watch it, boy!'

Oh, Dawu picked the tree for the canoe, but who cut the shape from the bark? Who flattened the bark over the fire, stitched the bark together at the bow and the stern, made the stitches watertight with hot beeswax? Only you, boy! Don't worry about waves and Lightning Serpents. This canoe swims like a whale.

Dawu turned with a frown. Yukuwa ducked his head, certain that Dawu had heard him thinking. But Dawu was looking over his head, at the beaches, as if he had forgotten something there.

Yukuwa followed his eye to the beach they had left, the lonely Kingfish Beach, then to the distant Beach of Trees, curving whitely to a distant clutter of rocks. There were only a few campfires there tonight.

Dawu slowly smiled. 'They're gone.'

Yukuwa nodded.

The Barra tribe has gone from the Beach of Trees. So Barra tribe's hairy boy has gone too. So Wanduwa will stop walking in his footprints, stop hovering round him like he was made of honey, and go back to being Dawu's wife. And Dawu might start being a hunter again and stop being a treeful of wasps.

'Hey boy?'

'Yes?'

'I say we're hunting. You don't listen.'

Yukuwa dipped his paddle and dragged a low wave past him, grinning a little.

All right, you don't understand Dawu's trouble with Wanduwa, no matter. Tonight the Barra tribe goes back to the mountain of Nhulunbuy, and tonight Dawu will find his eye again. *That* is important. Dawu's eye is worth a flight of kangaroos, a beach of turtles.

'Steady now.'

He's got something already! Maybe there *is* something down there, a turtle in the black deep.

But Dawu was looking ahead into the darkness of the night. Thunder rolled down on the canoe, but Yukuwa ignored it and tried to see with Dawu's eyes.

Can't see anything? You never could, but there is something out there now, because he can see it. Oh yes, he has struggled to teach you to see, got you to look for the wheeling gulls, the leaping fish, the rushing tide, the darkening of the water, all of that. But when he has finished, he can still point at a piece of sea thick with fish, and you can see nothing.

'Paddle softly. No turtle, but ...'

Dawu once tried to explain his fisherman's eye. 'Magic? No, I don't think so. I am not One-Eye and his demons. I am just an old man. Maybe I see a patch of sea, feel a wind, smell something in the air, and part of me remembers a time like that which gave me fish. I don't know ...'

But the fish were always there. The fish would be there this time.

Yukuwa looked away from the barren sea and down at the working paddle. And there *was* something there, something heavy, deep and black in the black water.

Yukuwa glanced at Dawu's back. Does he know about this? Of course he knows – if it is real. If it is not real it doesn't matter.

Lightning shivered to the sea, stilling the low waves a moment before the darkness flooded back.

'There!' said Dawu.

The phosphorescent trail of a big fish glowed dimly across the water. Dawu slid the canoe quietly along the track of the fish. He said something but thunder rolled over the words.

He lifted his paddle, pointed, and placed it beside him.

Yukuwa could see the motionless black hump in the water ahead and braced his knees against the bark sides of the canoe. No fish, but a mammal, a dugong. Better than a fish.

Dawu placed his hands gently on the edges of the canoe, his back humped, and he was standing. Yukuwa hardly felt the edges quiver against his legs as the bow nodded. Dawu had always been a fine dancer.

Now the canoe was sliding silently to the dugong.

Dawu waggled his finger before Yukuwa's face with a touch of impatience.

Yukuwa placed his paddle between his knees and lifted Dawu's harpoon, a shaved sapling with a spearhead carved from ironwood. He groped in the dark and felt the hook of the spear thrower, a shark's tooth. He slid the carved haft of the spear thrower along the harpoon until the tooth bit at the hollow of the harpoon's base, then passed the harpoon and the spear thrower, the woomera, to Dawu's waiting hand.

Dawu nodded once and slowly brought the harpoon back over his shoulder. He swung the thin line trailing from the spearhead out over the water as Yukuwa adjusted the coils of line before him.

A river of blue lightning shuddered to the sea, spreading until a skeletal tree stood on the water. Black cloud splintered apart. The night belonged to Lightning Serpents, not to little hunters and bark canoes.

'Soon,' Dawu whispered, as if he knew what his cowardly boy was feeling.

Yukuwa took his eyes off the light play in the sky and made a last slow stroke with his paddle.

Dawu reached back until the woomera was over Yukuwa's head, his left hand steadying the spear and controlling the line.

Yukuwa's tongue crept over his lip. The dugong is Dawu's. It is already on tomorrow morning's fire as certain as the rising sun! You can smell the roasted meat. Dawu can bring down a flying duck a hundred strides away and this dugong – bigger than a kangaroo – is so close you can hear it breathe.

Dawu was aiming the harpoon at the spine, behind the head. He would hurl the harpoon and the woomera would make his arm twice as long, twice as strong, as it unfolded from his arm. And to put all his power into the harpoon, Dawu would stay behind it as it left the canoe, stay with it until he fell into the water.

Dawu murmured, 'Good fish, good fish ...' Any moment now.

Yukuwa opened his hand and held the coils of the line clear of the canoe ...

He stared down past the coils. Something in the water.

A movement of black in the black water. A shadow sliding under the canoe, longer than the dugong, longer than the canoe.

'Dawu ...'

'No. Go away. It is between me and the fish.'

The shadow turned, showed the white of its belly. It was coming from the bottom of the sea.

'Dawu!' A shriek.

'No, boy!' shouting as the harpoon began to move.

The canoe lifted from the water, the harpoon left Dawu's hand. The bark sides of the canoe began to fold in, closing on his right foot. A loop of line flicked from Yukuwa's hand. Dawu's spear arm swung down, the woomera rearing, the harpoon flying at the torn sky. Water sprayed from the sides of the canoe and a hole ripped open in the bottom. A great hole, ringed with teeth.

Yukuwa was shouting. And falling.

2 RUNAWAY

Misty figures danced in the dark water.

A massive shadow whirled past Yukuwa, a carcass quivering in its mouth, a long body flopping against its side, boneless as seaweed. The shadow flicked a tall tail against his head, tumbling him. It jerked the carcass until it fell apart.

Yukuwa shook his head and his eyes cleared.

Oh . . .

A shark cruised round him, spitting bark. It swam away.

He kicked to the surface beside part of the canoe and gasped. Dawu. Where's Dawu?

Then he remembered the shark and forgot Dawu. He shoved his head back into the water. No shark, but the dim form of Dawu was limply drifting to the bottom of the sea.

Yukuwa looked again for the shark, squeezed his eyes shut, lifted his head and sucked in a breath. He dived quickly, too fast to think. He clawed himself down past streams of small fish to catch Dawu by his curly hair. He kicked towards the glimmer of the surface for a long time.

'All right?' Yukuwa panted.

Dawu coughed several times and started to breathe again, but he was unconscious and Yukuwa tasted something in the water around him.

Yukuwa held him at arm's length, looked at his arms, his shoulders, his hanging head. He ducked his head and looked at Dawu's body, his legs ... His right foot was staining the dark water black.

Yukuwa jerked his head out of the water.

Blood. The shark! It will smell the blood. Get out! Get away! It's coming back, now! Leave him ...

He saw the harpoon line and stopped.

No, it's gone away.

He stretched a trembling arm to the line and pulled in the harpoon. He slung Dawu's arms back over the half-canoe and reached for the injured leg. There were many, many little fish. The water was getting warmer, thicker as he reached. He lifted the leg.

No foot.

He dropped the leg back in the water and stared at the blood pumping silently among the little fish. He was beginning to shudder.

Stop it! Do something.

He clumsily tied the harpoon to Dawu's lower leg and turned the haft to tighten the line. The bleeding stopped. He tied the haft against the upper leg so it could not unwind.

No shark, see? What did you expect, after a taste of Dawu?

He felt strangely like giggling.

He caught Dawu's wrists, pulling him from the wreckage of the canoe. He turned and drew the man's arms over his shoulders until he could feel Dawu's jaw at the side of his neck.

'All right, teacher?' said Yukuwa, pinning Dawu's arms against his chest. He began to swim for shore.

It was a long swim. He could use only one tired arm and two short legs, with the Lightning Serpent writhing in the sky behind him.

After a while he began to worry about Dawu. 'Hey, are you still breathing?' he panted. 'Don't forget to breathe, father.'

Yukuwa lifted his head from the water and frowned. His words had somehow changed in the air.

Father. Fathers. Oh, you have many fathers, brothers of your real father. That is in the camp. But here in the dark water it is different. Dawu is more a father than the others. More than your real father ...

Yukuwa snorted. This crotchety old man, this lump on your back, this treeful of wasps, this teacher who worries more about his wife than his teaching. Father? Hah!

But he watched you on your first hunt, and he did not laugh when your spear missed. He was there when you found your first honey tree, taught you how to be a cockatoo in the dancing place. He told you about the spirit man who became the Moon and the secrets of the billabongs, showed you how to paint the stories on bark, taught you how to sing with the clapping sticks.

And before, when your fathers painted secrets on your body and women wailed and men danced, he cut you and you became a man. At eleven years ...

Yukuwa's foot scraped a rock and he staggered to his feet.

Dawu is a crotchety old man, but he is your teacher and sometimes your friend. He can't leave now. You hear?

Yukuwa dragged Dawu up the beach and looked around. 'Help! Help us, quickly!' he shouted hoarsely into the wind.

The beach was dark and empty, with sand whirling above the seaweed.

Come on, this is Kingfish Beach. No help here. You've got to leave Dawu and run to the Beach of Trees for help.

Yukuwa looked down at his trembling legs. Run? You can't walk faster than a crab now. If you leave Dawu he will die. What can you do?

Fire. You need a fire.

Yukuwa lowered Dawu to the sand and limped across the beach to the ashes of their morning fire. He found a stick with white ash clinging to the end and carried it back. A drop of water struck him on the face.

He shook his head and placed the branch under a ti-tree, then half carried, half dragged Dawu near its shelter. He bent over the man, and saw the sagging of his face, the leg oozing blood. But he was still breathing.

Yukuwa scooped dried bark and grass from under the tree and built a small mound around the end of the stick. He gently blew on the white ash until the black wood under the ash flared. The grass smoked, ignited, and the fire grew quickly.

But when Yukuwa turned, Dawu's breath had become shallow.

Yukuwa bit his lip. All right, all right. Don't stop. Get leaves.

He panted to the edge of the forest, stopped at a deep stream and snatched at the murgun vine, the big fleshy leaves that covered the bank. Then the hairy bark of the paperbark tree and some hanging strings. He ran back, but Dawu seemed to have stopped breathing.

'No!' Yukuwa shouted into the wind, skidding to his knees beside Dawu. 'Please ...'

And Dawu drew in a shuddering breath.

The rain swept up the beach and threatened the fire. Yukuwa scooped up a wall of sand against the wind and the rain, adjusted the fire and placed the murgun leaves near the flames. He raised Dawu's leg and washed it in the falling water.

He stared at Dawu's face and looked away. He began to sing out his desperation.

Do not take the spirit away.
Not with the blood
And the water.
It is not time.
It cannot be time yet.

He pulled on the skin of Dawu's leg until the skin covered the end of the bone. He tied the string to hold the skin in place. Dawu sighed through his teeth and shivered in the cold wind.

Yukuwa reached for the curling murgun leaves and plucked them from the flames. He juggled the hot leaves on the tips of his fingers and slapped them over the wound. Dawu gasped in pain, and shook.

He is dying. Father's dying, and I cannot do anything about it ...

Yukuwa began to wail into the rain and the storm.

Dawu coughed.

Not dead yet!

Yukuwa reached for more leaves and shouted for help. Dawu twitched as the new leaves bonded to the others in a tight bandage. His eyelids fluttered.

'Ho, help me!' Yukuwa yelled as he worked the paperbark in his hands. 'Help ...'

'Ho!'

Yukuwa turned from Dawu and squinted at the rain-swept beach. A figure was swirling from the edge of the forest. Too small for a full-grown man; a boy, like himself. It didn't matter. Yukuwa hung his head and his tension shivered along his arms. 'Ho,' he called.

'Hello brother ...' Ragan began his lopsided grin, then he saw Dawu, then Dawu's leg.

'Stupid shark thought the canoe was a dugong.'

'I can take over. You look worse than Dawu.'

Yukuwa began to move aside, to unload the responsibility. But Ragan was no older – they had shared the same initiation ceremony – and no wiser.

'All right, then?' Ragan squatted next to Yukuwa.

Yukuwa sagged but he shook his head. 'You better not, brother. You would have to wait for the Cleansing, like me. Better to keep on hunting.'

Ragan nodded and moved away.

'Get help, hey?'

Ragan raised his hand and slid back into the forest.

Yukuwa began to wind the paperbark around Dawu's stump. Then he stopped.

What have you done? Stupid boy, you know nothing. Ragan has learned everything, the spear, the dancing. He would know what to do. You have killed Dawu.

He turned to see Dawu's face, and one eye, half open, was fixed on him.

He's gone, gone away. Like the water running on the slope to join the sea ...

A very faint whisper. Dawu's lips moving over his teeth.

Yukuwa shuffled up the sand and lowered his head to Dawu's mouth. 'You are doing all right, I think.'

Yukuwa swallowed and flickered a weak smile at the man. He tried to say a few words, but something clogged his throat. Dawu closed his eyes, but his breathing was steady. Yukuwa shook his head and used the string that had hung from the tree to tie the bark to Dawu's leg.

He was still tying knots when several men slipped from the forest. Ragan reached him – he wasn't panting at all – then the men, the fathers and older brothers stepped past him.

'Ho,' Yukuwa said. It was over now. They would take over.

The hunters stood around him, leaning on their spears, while they looked at Yukuwa, at the fire, at Dawu and his leg and the harpoon. There was a short grunt and the hunters stepped aside.

Gathul moved forward. Yukuwa's real father had a deep trench between his eyes, streaks of white in his beard and well-worn authority.

'Well?' he said, as if he knew that this was Yukuwa's fault, and only wanted to have it confirmed.

Yukuwa started to tell Gathul about the shark and the sinking of his canoe and his swim to the beach, and the lighting of the fire ...

Gathul held up a hand. 'Dozy shark. We will eat him some time, I think.'

He squatted by Dawu's head and muttered something to him. Dawu moved his head uncertainly, but he stopped when Gathul rested a hand on his shoulder. 'Ragan? Get Wanduwa. Say that her husband needs her.'

Ragan nodded once and loped across the shadowy arc of the beach.

'Build up the fire. Get the bark. Come on. You know what to do.' Gathul clapped his hands and the hunters were gone.

Yukuwa carried a log back to the fire and saw Gathul examining his work on Dawu's leg. He felt a small glow when Gathul nodded once and left it be. Then Gathul lifted his head. 'I want you, son.' He motioned him to the harpoon tied to Dawu's leg.

'Brother? Dawu, can you hear me now?'

Dawu flickered his eyes and held them open.

'This will hurt.'

Dawu looked at Gathul, then beyond at Yukuwa with his hands on the harpoon. He shook his shoulders and coughed. It might have been laughter. 'That? Only that?'

Gathul nodded at Yukuwa.

Yukuwa sucked his lips and slowly turned the harpoon, easing the line around Dawu's leg above the knee, releasing the dammed blood to thunder down the leg, carrying with it a waking pain.

Dawu's eyes opened wide. His teeth clicked together many times, then he hissed like a dying lizard. The leaves and paperbark moved and darkened, but they held.

The hunters returned with slabs of bark, which they placed over the fire to flatten out.

Dawu clenched his fists at his sides, but after a while the fists relaxed and became hands again.

'Better, brother?' said Gathul, softly.

'Better.' Very weak, but he sounded settled.

Yukuwa leaned back limply and closed his eyes. It was over.

Spears were doubled for strength and the flattened bark was placed sideways over them. The hunters gently eased Dawu onto the bark, then gripped the ends of the spear-hafts and lifted the bark and Dawu into the air. They would walk beside him, carrying him on this stretcher across Kingfish Beach, to the Beach of Trees and to his shelter. The shark was gone and Dawu was surrounded by his brothers. He was safe.

But Ragan met them in the first hundred paces, with anger in his eyes. 'Wanduwa has gone!'

3 THE CLEANSING

Things started changing after that, but it took Yukuwa ten days to realise how much.

On the afternoon of the tenth day he was carrying some wood to the camp when he heard laughter and singing. He peered through the grey drizzle and saw some hunters sprawled under a needle-leaved casuarina tree. He wandered across – he couldn't join them while he was unclean, but there was nothing against him watching. Anyway, he was a bit of a hero and they might be singing a song about *him.*

Bawi, the long, lean hunter with the wispy beard, was singing like a mud frog, with Ragan playing Bawi's didgeridoo beside him. Ragan sucked and blew on the long hollow cylinder with his eyes closed, flicking at its side for rhythm, as if he was dreaming of a corroboree.

Bawi sang:

Lonely old man in his shelter,
Wondering where his wife can be ...

Then he noticed Yukuwa, and stopped. Ragan faltered, flicked his eyes open, saw Yukuwa and hunched awkwardly.

Yukuwa realised what he had heard and spun away in sudden anger. He banged blindly against One-Eye's grave-post, staggered a step, and stamped across the beach.

Not a corroboree, no. Ragan is playing for Bawi's gossip song so they can laugh at Dawu. Bawi laughing at Dawu! This is the great hunter who speared a wasp's nest, who hides from the Widow and rubs stuff in his beard to help it grow! Dawu should sing songs about Bawi ...

Yukuwa slouched past some children playing with the dingo pup in the shower-specked shallows and turned towards the shelters, high on the beach. Up there was Gathul in his shelter with a bunch of women standing around him in the rain. And Dawu sprawling sourly in his shelter.

Oh yes, Dawu is still sour, a bad-tempered pain in the neck ...

And you should not think things like that.

Hey, hey, hey. Why not?

It's not like the first days after the shark attack any more. Then nobody mentioned Dawu, frightened that saying his name might shake loose his spirit. Then most of the Wata tribe came and watched, left fish or crabs, and went away. Leaving you to do the rest, changing murgun leaves and paperbark on his leg, listening to him moan at night and mutter about Wanduwa in the day. Because only you have touched his wound.

But things are different now. Oh, until the Cleansing ceremony you're still stuck with Dawu like an oyster on a rock, but now nobody has to worry about him any more.

Yes, Dawu is a bad-tempered grouch. And now you can think things like that. People can even sing songs like that. He is getting better.

Seen like that, Bawi's gossip song is a good sign.

Isn't it?

@

Yukuwa moved his eyes from Dawu to Gathul's shelter and saw that something was happening.

Besides being Yukuwa's real father, Gathul was the head of the Wata tribe, a great hunter, and wise negotiator. When he sat in his shelter – a roof of branches and palm leaves held up by forked poles – he made it a special place just by being there.

But not now. Now he was surrounded by women, shouting at him, at each other. He was no longer a chief of hunters. He was only a listener, a camp dingo.

Yukuwa heard Wanduwa's name and stopped in the sand.

'Wanduwa should be punished.' That was Wapiti, Gathul's first wife. Heavy Wapiti. When she walked on the beach the sand squealed.

'I don't know ...' Quiet Duyga, second wife and Yukuwa's real mother, was propping a loaded gathering dish on her hip. Duyga was quiet and slow. Deliberately, so her thinking never stumbled.

'You don't know anything,' said Wapiti. 'She must be punished.'

'Why?'

'Show all the bad girls what's waiting for them.'

'What bad girls?' said the bony Widow. Most times she was a laughing widow, but now she was afraid.

'You don't think there are bad girls in the Wata tribe?' said Wapiti. 'You don't think Wanduwa is bad?'

'That's not fair, Wapiti,' said Duyga.

'Because the Widow is Wanduwa's mother? I would know what is good and bad whether I am a mother or a fish swimming in the sea.'

Gathul studied Wapiti.

Duyga sighed. 'What sort of punishment, Wapiti?'

'Kill her,' said Wapiti, and stabbed a stick into the sand.

'What?' said Duyga. The Widow made a choking sound.
'Yes.' Wapiti waved her hand in emphasis. 'It must be.'
'Why must it be?'
'It is the law. When a woman deserts an injured man – a man who cannot look after himself – that woman must die. It is the law.'
The Widow gave a soft shriek and scrambled to get away from the shelter, but Duyga caught her by the arm and held her.
'Yes ...' But Wapiti was looking at the Widow's face, her voice quivering slightly as she began to see the effect of what she was doing.
'I suppose ...' Gathul was slow and reluctant.
'But Wanduwa did not know!' Duyga shouted.
'Eh?'
'She left to follow that hairy boy when Dawu was out there hunting dugong. She could not possibly know that he had been attacked by a shark. You cannot kill her for that.'
Gathul scooped a handful of sand and allowed it to run slowly from his fist. 'I think Wanduwa must be brought back here.'
The women nodded.

Dawu was sitting up in his shelter, leaning against his turtle shell and cleaning the inside of a large crab claw. Yukuwa placed the damp wood near the smouldering fire, sat on his heels and stared at the sea.
'Well?' Dawu did not look up.
Yukuwa told him what he had heard.
'Kill her?' Dawu shook his head slowly.
'Mother stopped it. Father said she had to be brought back.'
'Yes, she must come back. She is a stupid little girl.'

Yukuwa looked at the children playing in the shallows and said nothing.

A handful of seasons ago, so close, you were out there, chasing little fish with a pointed stick, splashing Wanduwa. In just a handful of seasons Wanduwa had changed from a laughing girl pushing a toy boat to a wife Wapiti wanted to kill. And somehow she had turned Dawu from a great hunter into a heap of misery, and a gossip song. It didn't make sense.

Yukuwa shook his head. 'How's your foot?' he said.

'Better.' Dawu looked distantly at the end of his leg, and frowned. 'I can feel my toes. As if I'm still kicking at that shark's belly.'

Yukuwa lifted his eyes to the distant casuarina tree and the hunters with their gossip song. He felt a spark of anger.

And then he saw One-Eye's grave-post leaning towards him and the anger shrivelled into a twinge of alarm.

You have trampled over his memory, knocked his dignity sideways. *You may have woken his spirit.*

'Trouble?' said Dawu.

'No.' Keep calm. One-Eye mightn't have noticed. 'Maybe that shark had a bit of magic.'

'What magic?'

The grave-post was too far away to see the carvings and the faded colours, but Yukuwa felt it staring at him. 'Maybe a galka, a sorcerer, got some sorcery on that shark.'

Dawu looked past Yukuwa and saw the grave-post. 'He's dead, boy.'

Yukuwa nodded. Yes, you know that. That is why One-Eye's real name can never be spoken. His bones aren't under the grave-post, but in a painted hollow log by his symbolic waterhole. The grave-post is only to remind the tribe of him. But if his spirit has been disturbed maybe the galka can still cause trouble, bad trouble.

'Maybe the Barra tribe have a galka of their own,' he said.

'What? For the hairy boy? He has not got the wit of a rock. Magic is beyond him.'

And for the first time in ten days Dawu laughed. Laughed until his stump hurt. Yukuwa watched him in silence.

'I've been a bit of a problem,' Dawu said.

'It was all right,' Yukuwa said.

'But it will be better soon. When Wanduwa comes back.'

Dawu was crushing some blackened sand leaves into the bowl of the crab's claw when Duyga brought her gathering dish across from Gathul's shelter.

'Tonight, you feast!' Duyga grinned. 'Crabs, fish, shellfish ...'

'Good, good.' But Dawu sounded cautious. He picked a burning twig from the fire, lit the leaves and smoked them, using the claw as a pipe.

'Hello, mother.' Yukuwa smiled, but Duyga's returning smile was vague. Again there was something that he could not see.

Duyga squatted and nodded at the leaf-and-bark bandage. 'How is it?'

'Not bad.'

'It looks good.'

'Your son does a good job.'

Duyga did not even smile. 'This silly little girl ... '

'Wanduwa.'

'Her head is full of honey bees, eh?'

'Always. She burns yams.'

'She sings like a crow.'

'She dances like a one-legged man.' Dawu laughed.

Duyga nodded. 'So why do you want her back?'

The laughter died. 'I am good to her. I do not complain when she burns yams. I *eat* her burnt yams. I bring her dugong, wallaby, duck, even turtle.' He thumped the shell he was leaning on. 'Why does she leave me?'

'It happens.'

'But why?'

Duyga sighed. 'You are a good man, a great hunter. But maybe she is too young to see these things. Maybe you are too old for her.'

'Too old, too old? I am a baby. Gathul is the old one. He has too many wives.'

'Yes, well.' Duyga opened her hands.

'I only have one wife. I want her back.'

Duyga rose tiredly. 'We will bring her back after the Cleansing.'

Yukuwa watched his mother walk slowly back to Gathul's shelter. 'Is there going to be trouble?' he said.

'Put the crabs on the fire.'

One-Eye's grave-post leaned and watched Yukuwa.

But the post was forgotten when Bawi painted ochre bands on Yukuwa's arms and head. Yukuwa could not stop grinning. The days had trickled past like honey from a comb, but this was the Cleansing at last.

'Ho, what a lovely bird we have here!' Dawu swung up to Yukuwa on a forked branch. He too had been painted elaborately and could have been talking about himself.

It suddenly occurred to Yukuwa that Dawu was looking forward to the ceremony as much as he was. 'Ready to go fishing again?' he said.

'Yes ...' But Dawu's face fell a little.

'Stay still,' growled Bawi.

Yukuwa's totem, a raft, was painted on his belly, surrounded by symbols: waterholes, rivers, and old men's secrets. They showed that he was on the Yirritja side of the world. Every person, every child, every animal, fish, insect, reptile, every waterhole, creek, hill was either Yirritja or Dhuwa – either one side of the world or the other.

Yukuwa the Yirritja yam, he thought happily. Yukuwa of the Watu tribe of the Yolngu people, surrounded by special spirits and landforms to belong to. With many mothers, fathers, brothers and sisters. That is your exact place in life.

And you are about to be at the heart of a major corroboree for the second time in your life. And this time it won't hurt at all!

Yukuwa remembered the first time. It had started like this, with Ragan painted as well. A time of excitement, even laughter – then it changed. You could see Ragan's eyes darting about like a trapped wallaby.

But this time was different. He helped Dawu from the shelter to the dancing place on the beach in anticipation, instead of dread.

The first time the men had waved spears in the air and women had wailed for lost childhood.

But this time Duyga, Wapiti, the Widow – all the women of the tribe – danced before him, holding a twig or a piece of vine with both hands, their feet shuffling in the sand, sliding a little sand from one foot to the other. The women danced the gathering of Yirritja food, they danced to Gathul's Yirritja songs and the clapping sticks and Bawi's didgeridoo.

Yukuwa smiled at Bawi in satisfaction. No gossip song today, Bawi? Playing for Dawu now, in respect. That's better.

But the smile faded.

Remember the first time Bawi played for Dawu? When you were on a table formed by the chests of two fathers, and Dawu bent over with a sharp mother-of-pearl shell …

One moment you were a grim painted boy, then a slash – the circumcision – and you were a man. A man so proud that you did not shout at the pain, although Ragan did.

The smile flickered back to Yukuwa's face. He beamed at Ragan as he danced the hunting of kangaroos – a twitch of the nose, a jerk of the head to the right, to the left, the paws hooked before the chest and the short jump in the sand. I remember, I remember.

The Cleansing ceremony was very, very good, with the dancing and the singing, the low fires and the water in the large baler shells.

But it was over. Now Yukuwa could join the gossip songs under the casuarina and become a hunter again, and Dawu … Dawu would think of Wanduwa.

With a creeping dread Yukuwa watched as Dawu swung towards Gathul.

Gathul stood on the beach, staring at the wind-flattened sea. 'We must move soon, Dawu,' he said quietly, without turning his head.

'Why?'

Gathul nodded at the sea. 'They are coming. They are almost here.'

Yukuwa closed his eyes. Yes, remember your great turtle-shell, there's no time to wait …

But Dawu turned his back on the empty sea and shook his head violently. 'I want her back!'

Next morning Yukuwa watched Duyga, Wapiti and the Widow walk carefully past One-Eye's grave-post on their way to bring Wanduwa back.

4 THE PARTING

At first nothing happened.

Soon after the women left, Yukuwa sidled over to One-Eye's grave-post and tried to straighten it in the sand. It didn't move, but it creaked, a faint groan in his hands. He let it go and stepped back.

'Sorry, sorry.' He rubbed his hands nervously on his legs. 'I didn't mean to disturb you. It was an accident.'

That is no excuse, you know that. Wapiti tripped One-Eye once and later a snake bit her. Made her sick for two days. Now you have disturbed the galka, the sorcerer, and something has to happen. Maybe it is happening now.

Yukuwa wanted to go away but he sat in the sand, trying to work out something he could *do*.

He watched Dawu swinging down the beach with his spear and woomera. So today he does not want you. Great, dance in the sand.

But Dawu called One-Eye a venomous lizard just before he died. It wasn't the hairy boy who called the shark. It was One-Eye.

But One-Eye was dead.

Yukuwa rocked forward on the balls of his feet and closed his eyes. He is still there! There he is on the dark of your eyes! the way you first saw him, when you lay in a gathering dish. A fleshless face peering at you with a single eye. You yowled.

Once the galka had been no more than a hunter, but when he chased a lizard into a thorn bush he became One-Eye. He said he had been attacked by a galka from another tribe, so he must become a galka himself to avenge the eye. He went into the bush, slept on a man's grave and returned with something in his dilly bag. Later, a hunter in the other tribe became sick and died. One-Eye laughed and danced round his fire.

If One-Eye transfixed you with that terrible glittering eye and said you would die, you would die. One-Eye had caused Bawi's mother to be ill for six days after eating a fish he wanted. Gathul ignored One-Eye one day and later fell and broke his arm. One-Eye could have forced Wanduwa to return, but he wouldn't because he hated Dawu.

Last season, a galka from some other tribe came for One-Eye, sending a crocodile up on his blind side ...

Now he was dead.

Wasn't he?

'Ho, listening for the galka?' Ragan, leaning on a spear.

'I banged his grave-post.'

Ragan shrugged. 'What can you do? Come on, let's find a wallaby.'

Yukuwa pulled a face. That's Ragan all over: don't get frightened until it's chasing you, never worry if there's nothing you can do.

He followed Ragan into the bush and tried to forget about One-Eye.

You've been following Ragan into the bush since you started to walk, since chasing that great purple dragonfly into the swamp. 'Crocodile food, crocodile food!' Duyga had shouted then, slapping the ground to show how hard she wanted to beat your hide. But it was all worth it. Especially seeing a goanna – a mighty lizard – chase

Ragan up a tree. You would have helped him, but you were laughing so much.

Ragan once found a pair of brolgas courting in a shadowed glade and danced silently, copying the birds' ritual without disturbing them. The glade became his – and your – secret place.

'Ho!' Ragan tapped the trunk of a thin dead tree, pressing his ear against the wood. It had already lost its top, reducing it to a lonely pole.

'Bees?'

'Ants.' Ragan cut away at the base of the trunk with his flint spearhead, then he snapped it with a push. The crumbling heart spilled onto the grass. 'That's going to be a didgeridoo like Bawi's. Better than Bawi's.'

He picked up the trunk and pounded it on the ground to shake loose the rest of the eaten wood. He looked down the hollow cylinder, then suddenly looked up at Yukuwa. 'When did you bang One-eye's grave-post?'

'Long while ago. When you were singing about Dawu.'

'You were angry.'

'Yes.'

'About the song.'

'Yes.'

'We were only having fun.'

'Dawu was – is, *is!* – a great hunter. Best in the tribe. He shouldn't have gossip songs sung about him!'

'Bawi's song. I only play.' Ragan put his mouth to the trunk and it hummed. He shrugged and moved away.

Yukuwa sighed. Oh, Ragan is all right, just too good at too many things. But he still hasn't saved a man from a shark . . .

Yukuwa smiled and began hunting. Ragan found a fresh wallaby track and they slid silently apart. Then they found the wallaby, just like that, twitching away under the spiked leaves of a pandanus.

Ragan pointed to Yukuwa. He was to have the first spear. Welcome back, hunter!

Yukuwa eased a foot forward on the damp earth, drew back his woomera, the long spear swaying by his ear.

And his arm trembled slightly.

Oh, you had forgotten. But the arm remembers. Other hunters live for this moment. Lightning Serpents race along their veins. They are fast. They are accurate. They can do no wrong. But mud oozes along *your* veins ...

He stared at the wallaby, the twitching of its nose, the turning of its ears.

You are a good hunter – *if* you are with Dawu in the bark canoe, if someone else throws the spear ...

Yukuwa swept the woomera forward and down. And knew his spear would miss.

His spear hit the trunk of the pandanus and the wallaby spun toward Ragan. Yukuwa walked heavily to the pandanus and pulled the spear from the fleshy trunk.

Welcome back hunter? You never were one.

Yukuwa looked up to see Ragan apologising to the spirit of the wallaby twenty paces away. Ragan slung the carcass across his neck and used his bloody spear and the hollow trunk to pull himself to his feet.

'Well ...' Yukuwa was awkward.

Their eyes met for a moment, then skidded apart.

'You're just out of practice.'

They walked through the low forest, Ragan leading with his wallaby, the beginnings of his didgeridoo, and his lifted spear. Yukuwa trailing with his dipped spear, until they reached Kingfish Beach.

Dawu was standing in the shallows with his fishing spear.

They stopped in the shadows of the forest.

'I should have gone with him,' said Yukuwa.

'No, he didn't want you.'

'I should be there, helping.'

'No ...' Ragan squinted at Yukuwa. 'Why were you grinning at me?'

'I wasn't.'

'Not now, when I was dancing at the Cleansing ceremony.'

'Oh, I was remembering the other corroboree.'

Ragan watched Dawu lean on his crutch and slowly raise his spear.

'You mean when I yelled and you didn't.'

Dawu hurled his spear into the water. His crutch reared like a bird's wing and he fell backwards with a splash.

'Can't even throw a spear. He's even worse than you!' Ragan laughed and walked towards the camp.

Yukuwa watched Dawu sit up in the water. He rolled over, propped the crutch before him and pulled himself up on to his foot. He lurched through the water, stopped, shrugged and picked up his fishless spear. He raised the spear to his shoulder, stood one-legged and waited for another fish and another attempt.

Yukuwa turned away and followed Ragan. They skirted Kingfish Bay, passed One-Eye's grave-post and reached the camp.

On the second day the hunting stopped. Yukuwa heard that Bawi had been talking about Wanduwa and the Barra tribe and the hunters had listened. He found Bawi sitting on a log working on a spearhead.

'No hunting today?' asked Yukuwa.

'No. No time.'

'What're you doing?'

'Sharpening spears.'

'For wallabies?'

'For Barra.'

'But they camped with us. They were friends.'

'That was before they stole Wanduwa. Before we sent our women to steal her back.'

'What will they do?'

'Don't know. Maybe they don't want us to steal Wanduwa back. Maybe you better practise with your spears.' Bawi scratched the spear scar high on his leg. Yukuwa remembered that Bawi had once killed a man.

Yukuwa found Ragan hurling spears at a distant tree.

'I don't know what we're doing,' Ragan said weakly. 'I don't want to throw spears at people.'

'It could happen?'

'Yes. You're lucky.'

'Why?'

'When I throw they expect me to hit something.'

Yukuwa sat with Dawu under his shelter on the third day. They watched the metal fish prongs being honed, flint being carefully chipped for new edges, new spears being made, spears being constantly lodged in woomeras and hurled down the beach.

All this for the Barra tribe.

But to Yukuwa the Barra were just a distant part of his family. Even the hairy boy who stole Wanduwa. They were all of the Yolngu people, with the same customs, the same dancing, the same Dreaming, almost the same words. When they met they hunted together, ate together, married each other ...

You can't fight people like that.

'It can't be that bad, can it?' Yukuwa said.

Dawu turned away.

In the evening Yukuwa went to One-Eye's grave-post. He knelt in the sand and opened his hands. 'Please ...' he whispered.

But he knew it was useless.

On the morning of the fourth day Duyga and Wapiti walked into the camp and watched the spears being sharpened. Gathul motioned them over.

'Big hunt?' Wapiti said.

'Did you bring her?'

'Back there. With the others.'

Gathul's spear lifted from his leg. 'Barra? How many?'

'Not many, the hairy boy, two of his fathers, a brother. They don't want trouble.'

'But the boy wants Wanduwa,' said Duyga.

'They want trouble.'

'Perhaps ...' Duyga came to Dawu's shelter and motioned Yukuwa away. She squatted next to Dawu and he offered his crab-claw pipe as they talked.

Yukuwa watched his mother lean intently towards Dawu, with her eyes locked on his. You've seen her like this, when she wants to use her little magic. When she is telling a story from the Dreaming she will use her eyes and voice to wash out the world and wash in myths of kangaroos becoming men. Now she is slowly washing an idea, a truth, over Dawu. Maybe something to end a battle before it begins ...

But suddenly Dawu shook his head violently. He hopped to his foot and glared down at Duyga. He shouted, 'Bring her to me!'

Duyga stood and faced him for a moment of last appeal. Then she walked through the camp to the trees. Wapiti followed her.

Yukuwa looked dully at his spear. The fighting must come now.

Dawu swung onto the open beach and stood with his crutch and spear, waiting.

Gathul walked over to him, squeezed his shoulder and stood beside him with his metal spearhead glinting in the sun. The hunters straggled across the sand with their spears. Bawi propped three spears in front of him; Ragan stopped behind him, his eyes locked on the trees. Yukuwa placed his spear in his woomera and wished he was with the shark.

The hairy boy stepped out of the trees and stopped.

He didn't look so hairy now. There was an explosion of long hair on top, yes, but under that a very frightened boy was trying to look tough.

Yukuwa nodded slightly. You know *exactly* how he feels.

Dawu glared at the boy as the other men from the Barra tribe, a nervous handful, moved behind him. The women stepped past them: Wapiti casual, she'd done all that was expected of her; the Widow, the mother, desperate, with her eyes welling; and Duyga, sagging and tired. She had tried and lost.

Wanduwa stepped through the women, saw Dawu and faltered. The women had put a ring of possum skin and parrot feathers in her hair, showing that she would come back if Dawu wanted her. But she had been crying.

Dawu lurched across the sand, swinging his spear, watching Wanduwa's face. She stared at Dawu's gait, then at his shortened leg. 'I ... I didn't know ...'

Dawu stopped, his eyes switching from Wanduwa to Duyga and back again. He shook his head and thrust his spear at Wanduwa's head.

He cut a lock from her hair, snatched at the feather and threw it onto the sand. 'Go, go. Don't bother me.'

He turned and stamped away.

Wanduwa watched him go, raising uncertain fingers to her hair, slowly realising that she had been set free. A spark flickered in her eyes, but her face did not change on the long walk back to the boy.

Duyga sagged weakly, but Yukuwa thought he saw the glimmer of a smile.

Gathul clapped his hand on Yukuwa's shoulder. 'That's it, then.'

Yukuwa lifted his eyes to One-Eye's distant grave-post in slow surprise. That's it? There's nothing more? Then you are really dead.

'Tomorrow we go to meet the sea people,' said Gathul.

5 THE WALKABOUT

Next morning Dawu was stroking his turtle shell as he stared at the horizon.

Yukuwa moved closer to him. 'They'll give you many things for this.' He ran his fingers over the shell.

'I think so.' Dawu clicked his mouth and pounded Yukuwa on the shoulder. 'Time to think of new things. Of sea people and smoking houses and grey worms!'

'The Macassans!' Yukuwa beat a fast rhythm on the shell. Forget Wanduwa. Soon she would be no more than a memory.

A little later the Widow came over to Dawu's shelter and tapped on the shell. 'I'll carry this for you.'

Dawu and the Widow looked at each other, then he nodded.

The bony woman lifted the great shell with a soft grunt, putting it on her head.

Gathul came by with a few hunters, clicking his fingers at Yukuwa as if in a sudden thought. 'Son, you look after the firestick.'

Yukuwa began to grin at his father's retreating back – a very important job, given to him! Then he saw the touch of disappointment in Dawu's face.

Oh yes. The boy with the firestick can't hunt. Gathul

was saying that you are not wanted as a hunter, even with Dawu's teaching.

Yukuwa watched the hunters walk from the camp into the forest, carrying only their spears and woomeras. Hunters were always first, with no load, as they must always be ready for game. Ragan was already hefting his spear as if he expected a kangaroo to leap from behind the next tree. Hunters were always the leaders of the tribe ...

But you're not one. You were a small hero for a little while, but that's gone now.

The women followed the men, carrying their digging sticks, their gathering plates, dilly bags, the baler shells filled with fresh water and some food gathered yesterday. Wapiti strode under her load, showing the importance of the tribe's Number One wife, but Duyga gossiped with the Widow as if they were just looking for yams. Duyga smiled at Yukuwa as the children and the dingo pup scampered around them.

'All right, boy!' Dawu waved the crutch from the edge of the forest. Yukuwa hurried from the shelter, then scuttled back for a heavy piece of wood smouldering from last night's fire. The firestick.

He looked around at the shelters standing high on the beach with the black smudges of dead fires on the sand; a couple of grinding stones for seeds; the broad spread of shells, bones, vegetable scraps; the canoes, dragged up to the trees and tethered to a trunk; One-Eye's grave-post.

And that's it. You spend a couple of moons here, grow a bit bigger, but you don't become a better hunter. You go around being scared of Lightning Serpents, a shark, a war that never was and a dead sorcerer. And looking after the father who was supposed to look after you. Are you sad to leave?

Oh, you'll be back after a few moons. The canoes will have been wrecked by ants and animals after the honey wax, the roofs of the shelters blown away. But the camp will have been swept clean by rain, wind and king tides. There will be nothing here but the grinding stones, the frames of the shelters and the grave-post. The campsite will be fresh, ready to live in again. Not sad at all.

Yukuwa turned from the Beach of Trees and followed Dawu.

Gathul led the tribe inland, away from the coast and towards the Swamp as the forest darkened under heavy cloud. Yukuwa began to realise that by tonight his firestick could be the tribe's most precious possession.

The forest now glowed with fresh, luminous green. Paperbarks, ironwoods heavy with new foliage, pandanus and cycad palms reared for the filtered grey light. Long grass shoots, bushes and big-leaved round yam fought for ground space – and waited.

'What are you so happy about, boy?' Dawu was slowly moving apart from the tribe, brooding by himself.

But Yukuwa was listening to the last rain's slow dripping. He was smelling damp earth, soaked bark and the bitter whiff of wet charcoal. 'Happy? Who's happy?'

'We are going to get very wet.'

Nobody can light a fire without us, thought Yukuwa smugly, blowing on the firestick.

The Lightning Serpents played across the black sky as the sleeting flood shook the trees. Gathul talked of making a shelter of pandanus leaves until the storm passed overhead, but Duyga told him he was being an old woman.

Yukuwa felt rushing water round his feet as he walked down a gentle slope. Dawu wobbled many times and Yukuwa thought of moving nearer to steady him, but that would put the firestick at risk. He stayed away until

Dawu stopped with the hunters at the edge of the Swamp.

In the dry season the swamp would tick with lazy insects as clusters of birds settled on the still water. But now the swamp was part of a flood plain, water rushing through the new green grasses to the sea. An explosion of red and green became a flight of rainbow lorikeets, twisting in the air. Black cockatoos flared their red tails as they attacked the grass seeds. Two jabirus spread their wide grey wings and coasted over the swirling water. One peeled off to pluck a fish from the flooded grass.

Gathul clapped his hand on Dawu's shoulder. 'You'll do well, wawa, brother.'

Dawu flinched, but he followed the hunters into the flood.

Yukuwa stayed with the women and the children on the high ground, watching. He could hear Dawu's crutch sucking at the mud.

Ragan turned his head quickly to grin at Yukuwa. He was pointing at a large goanna sliding through the water. He threw his spear, the goanna thrashed briefly and sank. Bawi disturbed a file snake, but his spear skidded off its back. He ran after it, splashing and laughing, and panicked a treeful of black cockatoos. They flew low at Gathul, who thrust his spear blindly into the whirring confusion and brought one down.

And Dawu threw his spear in a long arc, jerking, swaying, falling to his knees while the spear was still in the air. The spear sliced into the water and something silver splashed. Dawu fought to his foot and lurched towards his spear before the fish broke free.

But Bawi abandoned his snake to fall upon Dawu's fish, stabbing with his spear. He held up a silver barramundi as long as his arm and shouted in triumph.

Dawu stopped hurling himself across the Swamp and stood tiredly in the water.

After the hunters, the women found a few goose and duck eggs, and a gang of children almost caught a flapping, honking goose. Duyga caught Bawi's file snake, killing it by holding its head between her teeth and jerking its body down.

Yukuwa built the firestick into a very smoky fire on the low rise Gathul declared a campsite. The fire became a pool of glowing coals and Gathul threw his cockatoo at the last flickering flame. Ragan tossed his goanna beside it, Wapiti and some older children placed the eggs carefully on hot ashes, Duyga draped her rough-skinned file snake on the coals.

Then Bawi placed the barramundi in the centre of the coals. Dawu looked at the fish without expression but he accepted the steaming piece Bawi offered.

'Our fish, eh?' said Bawi.

'Yes. Our fish.'

Dawu didn't talk much that night. He slept apart from the wriggling humps of the families.

In the morning a little girl found a larrani tree near a creek and squealed at the sight of the small shiny apples. She realised what she had done and clapped her hand across her mouth as she looked up, but far too late. All the children in the tribe galloped, scurried, shrieked down the slope to her and her tree. She yelled at them, hit at them, and was trampled in the rush. She managed to grab only three apples before they left the tree bare.

'Insects!' she shouted after them.

Everyone laughed – everyone except Dawu.

The tribe reached the edge of the thick river mangroves but only Duyga and three women took their digging sticks into the gnarled net of roots. On the other side of the mangroves was the tribe's target, Old People's Camp, but it would be far easier and quicker to go around.

The tribe moved along the edge of the mangroves, but Dawu fell behind, now panting, wobbling on his crutch. Yukuwa stopped practising his Macassan words and waited for Dawu.

'What do you want?' Dawu's brow was dripping sweat.

'Can I help?'

'No. I don't need anyone.'

Yukuwa walked on, but stayed close.

They caught the tribe at the river crossing. The mangroves and the salt water had given way to a rush of muddy fresh water. Wapiti and other women were cutting paperbark from trees for small canoes to carry babies and dilly bags.

'We're nearly there,' Yukuwa tried. But Dawu had stopped on a rise. Duyga bustled past, showing him mud crabs from the mangroves, but he did not notice. He was watching Gathul with pain in his eyes.

Gathul was standing on the edge of the river, pointing at the mud slides and the grey shapes on the banks, talking to Bawi.

'Counting crocodiles?' Yukuwa said.

'The river's still shallow. There are four crocodiles down there, but they are surrounded by food ... Gathul is asking Bawi for advice.'

Yukuwa watched in silence.

'I think ... You better go round with Bawi in future.'

Yukuwa looked down at his spear. He swallowed. 'All right.' He took a step. 'I was trying to get better ...' and turned his back.

'What? Boy, what are you talking about?'

'I'm not a very good ...'

Dawu threw back his head in laughter. '*You!* You've

got it all wrong!' He sobered. 'No, you're all right, boy. It's *me.*'

'What's wrong with you?'

Dawu looked at Yukuwa. He wanted to say something, but other words came out: 'How can I teach you things that I cannot do myself?'

'You hit the fish, not Bawi.'

'What's the good of hitting anything if you can't follow it up, if you can't take it in your hands. No, you would be better with Bawi ...'

'No.'

'No?'

Yukuwa surprised himself. Suddenly Dawu was far more than the old grouch. It was as if they were back in the storm at Kingfish Beach. 'I want to stay with you. Bawi is nothing. You know more than he'll ever know.'

Dawu's eyes flickered uncertainly. 'Well, maybe.' He turned to the river and then began to smile. 'Come on.'

Yukuwa stumbled after Dawu with wide eyes. He *knew* what Dawu was going to do.

They reached the bank of the river as Bawi was pointing out the dull grey forms of three crocodiles sunning themselves on the bank.

'They're not hungry,' said Dawu as he swung into the river.

Yukuwa brushed past Bawi with arms rigid. He took one great step into the river ...

Bawi and Gathul, shamed by Dawu's rush, charged past him with a yell and a splash. Then Ragan, and the hunters, and Duyga and all the women with their little canoes, and the children and the dingo pup. One crocodile showed brief interest in the din, then climbed onto its mud slide and watched. Yukuwa waded out of the river with a grin, but a small shiver stayed with him for a long time.

The tribe laughed through a forest and over some hills. Yukuwa stayed with Dawu, talking, joking, sometimes in Macassan, and looking at the firestick in his hands. He began to wonder if Gathul had given him the firestick just to keep him with Dawu ...

In the evening they walked down to the sea. Near oyster cliffs, ragged shelters sagged under casuarina trees, facing an open bay. A rocky headland held a small sapling to a low moon. A Macassan sapling, a tamarind tree.

Old People's Camp was waiting.

6 THE MACASSANS

Yukuwa woke before the sun, with the back of his neck prickling. What is it? Dawu is snoring at your feet, looking almost happy. Gathul is sprawling under his shelter with Duyga and Wapiti. A seagull is pecking casually around the fire. No, there is nothing here.

But something ... something out there.

The sky was quiet, drained of the night's fury and left with only a smear of tinted cloud. The sea was motionless, like a shining moon. As if everything was fresh, incomplete, as if the bay had not existed yesterday.

It was from the Dreaming.

When Duyga told stories from the Dreaming it was like this. Before people were made and the Djang'kawu Sisters and their Brother came across the rain-soaked sea ...

Yukuwa stood up and felt the grains of sand tumble down his legs. A light movement of air brought the scent of sea salt – and a taste that tickled the back of his nostrils, something hot and heavy.

The rim of the sun nudged the horizon, washing the sea in gold.

There was a boat, a proud boat with great seagull wings, coming out of the sun.

As if the Sisters were coming to the land with their

sacred mat and dilly bag to create the first people. Coming again.

Yukuwa stood on the quiet beach for a long time, holding the vision like a bubble in his hands. Until Bawi sat up, squinted and yelled. 'The Macassans!'

Yukuwa sighed and stoked the fire into life, and the rest of the camp grunted awake. Dawu tossed yesterday's fish onto the coals, Duyga took her digging stick to the cliffs for oysters, Bawi and Ragan waded into the sea for some fish. Gathul groped around Wapiti's dilly bag for the brightly patterned sarong the Macassans had given him the last time they were here, and put it on.

The boat moved slowly into the arms of the bay.

It seemed bigger every time it came – longer than four canoes, and a man standing in a canoe could just reach the deck. On the deck there was a large shelter for a tribe that wandered the sea instead of the land. The shelter was covered in humps, like the back of a great crocodile. Above this were three tall trees, tied together at the top to hold the great seagull wings. The wings were trying to fly away with the wind.

But the Macassans were reducing their boat from the Dreaming to a great log. The top wing was hauled down, rolled until it was no more than a long branch and tied to one of the trees. The trees became thick poles. The last wing fluttered and died.

Yukuwa ran down to the water and waved. No more magic, but the Macassans are here, with wonders from their boat, tales from beyond the sea, strange tastes, strange songs, moons of adventure!

He waited impatiently for them to step ashore.

An anchor was dropped from the bow and about twenty men waved from the roof of the shelter. But they made no move to leave the boat.

Yukuwa frowned. This was the third time he'd seen

the Macassans, but it was the first time he'd watched them arrive. He was surprised that they were so slow.

One man placed a steaming metal plate on a large tray and another man added a bottle and a cup. The captain said something and the men stood on the deck. Two men lowered the tray on a rope into the sea.

Yukuwa understood: Ragan apologises to the wallaby's spirit after spearing the wallaby; Duyga leaves a few yams in the earth to make peace with the spirit of the yam place. The Macassans are offering a fine meal to the spirit of the sea for a good harvest.

The men then lifted humps from the shelter and dropped them in the sea, now canoes. A fleet of eight canoes surrounded the boat, filled with shouting, laughing men. They paddled furiously for the shore.

The tribe gathered on the beach, the women holding pieces of bark before them, waving and shouting welcome. But Yukuwa saw Dawu stroking his beard, as if he could see something the rest of the tribe could not.

'We could do that,' Dawu said.

Yukuwa recognised the Macassan captain, Laba, from last time, but this time he had a boy in his canoe. Two men thrust their canoe in front of Laba and one of them, a squat man, flashed his red teeth. But the other, a sleepy youth, stopped paddling when he saw Laba's glare. Red Teeth muttered angrily at Sleepy as Laba's canoe slid onto the sand. The boy jumped from Laba's canoe in triumph – to trip over Red Teeth's paddle and tumble into the shallows.

Yukuwa snorted back a tickle of laughter, but Red Teeth was snickering.

The boy kicked himself angrily to his feet, started to shout at Red Teeth but stopped when he saw Yukuwa's twitching face. He dragged the canoe hard onto the sand.

Laba stepped from the canoe and moved towards

Gathul. Yukuwa was surprised at how alike they were. Not at first glance: Laba wore everything – a cloth on his head, a shirt, a bigger cloth slung over his shoulder, slightly ragged trousers, a thick leather belt and a knife. Gathul wore only the Macassan sarong and he wore that because Laba was there. Laba was brown, Gathul was black; Laba was short, Gathul was tall.

But they both had faces like cracked mud, with a bit of white speckling their hair. They both smiled as if they were the best of friends, but they were watching each other like hunters measuring prey.

Gathul clapped his hands on Laba's shoulders. 'Welcome back to Marege, brother!'

Yukuwa smiled. He is being very polite. He does not welcome them to the Land of the Yolngu, he uses the Macassan name.

'It's good to be back, wawa, my brother.' Laba spoke the Yolngu words but with a strange, drifting accent.

'Did you sell well?' Gathul was speaking Macassan words.

Laba snapped his fingers and the boy scampered back to the canoe, lifting a heavy bundle wrapped in gold and black material. He placed it at Gathul's feet and stepped sideways to face Yukuwa.

'We did well, brother. We *all* did well.' Laba unwrapped the bundle.

Gathul squatted and handled the new material, some flashing with silver: knives, iron spearheads, tomahawks, tobacco and two long pipes.

'That is good.' He passed one of the spearheads to Bawi, not to Dawu.

Bawi pricked his finger with the spearhead and nodded.

Yukuwa felt Dawu stiffen beside him. But Dawu wasn't looking at Bawi, but at Sleepy. The youth was standing at the edge of the water and staring at Dawu's stump.

'And we have brought rice and flour,' said Laba.
'And we have fish, mud crabs and oysters. We will have a feast!'
Other Macassans were carrying bags onto the beach, but Sleepy had not moved.
'So?' Dawu was leaning forward on his crutch, his face hardening.
Sleepy looked up and fumbled. 'Oh, ah, Gali, that's me.'
'So?'
Gali pushed hair back from his face. 'What happened?'
'Shark. It wanted a bit of me.'
'But not too much.'
Dawu studied Gali's face, then shrugged. 'No, not too much.'
'I am sorry.'
Yukuwa heard sand crunching near him and turned to find the boy glaring at him. He wore a shirt, a knife and a dark green sarong wrapped round his legs almost to the knees. How could he move at all?
'You think everything is funny, eh?' said the boy.
'Ah, no,' said Yukuwa.
'Just me, eh?' said the boy and he grasped the handle of his knife. 'You think I am funny.'
Yukuwa watched the boy; the darting eyes, the tense body, the flash of metal as he lifted the knife a fraction. Then he saw the trickle of blood on the boy's knee. 'Why did that man trip you?' he asked.
The boy glanced down. 'That is mad Madya. I will not forget.' But he flicked his eyes back to Yukuwa. 'You think I am funny.'
Yukuwa sighed. 'Yes, I think you are funny.'
The boy blinked. 'Well, so are you!'
Yukuwa shrugged. 'Yes, I know.'
The boy took his hand awkwardly from his knife. 'Well, all right. What's your name?'

'Yukuwa.'

'Yuck-oo-wah.' The boy tasted the name. 'Sounds like food.'

'It means a yam. My mother found a yam cluster when I was born.'

'My name is Jago,' the boy said. 'I am related to a king.'

7 JAGO

Next day the work began. Crazy work. Yukuwa and Jago towed a canoe along the shallows to pick up sea slugs; like huge snails without shells, long, fat and grey, with the feel of leather eggs. Yukuwa remembered nibbling one of these – once. He had to chew grass to get rid of the taste. Nobody he knew ever *ate* them.

But the Macassans called them trepang and came to the Land of the Yolngu just for them. So Yukuwa filled a bucket in Jago's canoe with sea slugs he didn't want. Crazy work, like Duyga gutting them on the beach, Dawu boiling them, and Gathul cutting bamboo to build a house for them!

But it isn't that bad, Yukuwa thought. Maybe the worst of it is that Dawu isn't hunting with you, that he is with sleepy Gali, and you are stuck with this funny boy.

Jago glared at Yukuwa. 'What are you looking at?'

'You're bleeding.' Yukuwa pointed at Jago's knee.

Jago shrugged. 'Must've banged it. It's open again.'

'Maybe you should dry it in the sun.'

'All right.' Jago climbed into the canoe. '*You* pick up trepang.'

Yukuwa threw two trepang into the second bucket.

'I am going to get him,' Jago muttered, hunched over his knee.

'Who?' Yukuwa looked closely at Jago's knee.

'Mad Madya.' Jago patted his knife, then he looked up and pulled his leg away. 'Are you a savage?'

'What's a savage?'

'My mother says you are all savages,' said Jago.

'She has been here?'

'She has never left Macassar, but she knows everything.'

'What's a savage?'

'Oh, they're black, like you ...'

Yukuwa looked at Jago. This poor boy is only deep brown, like ironwood. Macassar must be a long way west, where the sun goes at the end of the day and it is too tired to burn people a proper black.

'And they don't wear anything.'

'Why?'

'Why what?'

'Why do you wear things?'

'Because we are not savages.'

'Yes, and you eat these.' Yukuwa waved a trepang at Jago, squeezing a squirt of water from it.

Jago ducked. 'We do not!'

'You don't?'

'Never!'

'Then why do you come here and spend the wet season getting them and cooking them?'

Jago looked wise. 'For the men from China.'

'China? Another tribe?'

'Sort of. They come to Macassar in a huge ship, the Great Junk, once a year. They bring painted plates, lanterns, silk, scented wood, and they take our trepang. Laba says they take them home and put them into soups. And eat them. I don't know how they do that!'

'They must have terrible food to eat in China,' Yukuwa said.

'Yes ...' Jago watched Yukuwa carefully. 'Mother says

savages eat people. Do you eat people?'

Yukuwa looked at Jago's skinny legs. 'I'd rather eat trepang – raw.'

Jago rocked back and laughed. A smile flickered across Yukuwa's face, then he joined Jago in the laughter. He couldn't understand it.

Eventually Jago stopped and studied Yukuwa.

'What's wrong?'

'You're not a real savage,' said Jago in disappointment. But then he looked at the headland and smiled slowly. 'But there's still Madya.'

Yukuwa grunted. This boy is a little crazy.

'C'mon.' Jago clapped his hands.

'There's room for more trepang.'

'That's enough. Let's go!'

Yukuwa bounced from the sand into the canoe and Jago paddled furiously towards the headland. Yukuwa echoed Jago's strokes and was surprised at the speed of the heavy wooden canoe. The outrigger was hissing through the water beside them like a fish.

As they scudded the canoe up onto the beach, Duyga took one of the buckets. 'All you men do is play,' she muttered, carrying the bucket to the cluster of women who were cleaning the trepang with Macassan knives.

Children ran up the beach with the gutted trepang, shrieking as they threw them into bubbling dishes.

'*They* are playing. We're not,' said Yukuwa.

'Come on, no time!' said Jago.

But Dawu waved as they neared the bubbling dishes. 'Swap you jobs,' he said.

Dawu was feeding the fire under the dishes. They were deep, wide enough to boil his giant barramundi, and made of iron. They were held in a thick bamboo frame over a trench lined with flat stones and filled with fire.

He had been working on the fire for half a day and sweat was pouring from him.

'If you want.' Yukuwa said, but he did not want that job. At all.

Dawu looked back at the sleepy youth who was stirring a dish with a long ladle. 'Like to take the canoe out, Gali?'

Gali shook his head slowly. 'Rather lie in the shade.' He added shreds of mangrove bark to the boiling water and the water swirled red.

Dawu shrugged at Yukuwa. 'No, you can have it.'

'Hurry!' Jago snapped his fingers and walked rapidly up the hill – backwards. Yukuwa followed, opening his hands to Dawu as if he did not know what was going on.

But his face was tight. Any moment now this crazy boy will do something stupid and you are going to get involved.

'Where's Madya?' Yukuwa stepped over the freshly boiled and buried trepang to get near Jago.

'Shut up! Turn round, walk backwards.'

Yukuwa turned. He's going to pull out that knife of his and wave it at Madya. You have to stop him. Where is Madya?

He looked over his shoulder at the high skeletal shelter. There was a short man working on the framework of the roof.

'Don't look,' Jago hissed.

Yukuwa straightened and kept walking backwards with Jago.

Stop him. Jump on him, push him into the ground. No, no. Better do it like Duyga. Talk, get him talking instead. But what about? You can't tell him he's stupid.

Below, Dawu was swinging towards the canoe as Gali watched him thoughtfully, the scoop with a reddening trepang drooping from his hands.

'Ah, does the bark make the trepang taste better?'

Yukuwa asked Jago. *That* is stupid. You have to do better than that.

Jago looked sideways at Yukuwa. 'You are trying to stop me.'

'You are going to get hurt ...'

'It is to fool the Great Junk.'

Yukuwa was surprised and stumbled. 'How do you fool a boat?'

'The people on it, rockhead. There are many different trepang. White is no good, it is coarse.' Jago was rubbing his hands on his sarong. 'The grey here is better but the Great Junk likes red more – so we give them red ...'

Yukuwa tried to recover. 'Doesn't matter. You leave Mad ...'

Jago broke away and sprinted for the trepang house. Yukuwa reached for him, clutched air and raced after him.

'Jago!' Yukuwa yelled.

Madya stood on the bamboo frame of the roof and looked down.

Jago slapped his hands round one of the uprights. 'When we Macassans build anything, it is strong – even for trepang. See?'

He shook the bamboo violently, heaving, grunting until the framework around him swayed and shivered.

'Hey!' Madya swayed on the roof, waving his arms about.

Yukuwa grabbed Jago's hands to pull him away from the bamboo.

Madya shouted and toppled from the roof with several pieces of bamboo. To splash into a puddle.

'Oops,' said Jago, and grinned.

Madya staggered to his feet and fumbled for his knife.

Jago's grin vanished. He stumbled backwards. 'I was only ...'

'Hey! Hey, Madya!' Gali was running up the hill, pointing his ladle.

Madya had drawn his knife, his kris, with a long blade that rippled like the sea, and he was moving after Jago.

'Don't be a bloody fool!' Gali flung his ladle.

Madya hesitated and watched it turning in the air. He stepped aside, allowing the ladle to splash into the puddle. 'Fighting with spoons now, Bugis?' He spat the last word.

But Gali slowed and smiled. 'Only stopping a little trouble.' He walked between Madya and Jago, picked up his ladle and clouted Jago across the ear with it, almost accidentally. 'You don't want to get stirred up by the Captain's boy, eh?' And he walked back down the hill.

Madya looked at his kris in faint surprise. He lifted the glittering blade, not to Jago but to Yukuwa. 'Monkeys,' he said. 'I skin monkeys.'

But it was over. He put his kris away and climbed up the trepang house and Jago went back to the canoe, holding his ear.

'He shouldn't have done that,' Jago muttered.

'I think he saved you,' said Yukuwa.

'From Mad Madya?' Jago drew his own kris from its sheath. 'I would have killed him.'

He stabbed the air.

And he calls Madya mad, Yukuwa thought.

8 DAWU'S FOOT

Yukuwa waited tensely for the next flare-up all the next day. And the next, and the next. A new moon came and went and nothing happened.

Gali played strange music on a coconut after the day's work; Madya had long, loud arguments with the Macassan holy man, Tale, but he never pulled his knife; and Jago joked and learned to dance the wallaby, never mentioning Madya's name. Old People's Camp was busy, but peaceful.

Until Dawu got his foot.

Yukuwa was squatting under a casuarina tree with Ragan, listening to the patter of rain on the leaves and to Tale singing in the Macassan camp. Tale sang from the painted leaves of a 'book' and when he had finished Ragan played his finely painted didgeridoo to Yukuwa's clapping sticks. Jago came over from the Macassan camp.

'What's happening?'

Yukuwa stopped. 'Me and wawa, we are making a song.'

'In Macassan. It is very hard,' Ragan said.

'What is "wawa"?'

'It means brother,' said Yukuwa.

'Like your fathers? You have many brothers?'

'Oh yes. You can be my wawa.'

'No.' Jago shook his head. 'I am not your wawa.'
Yukuwa shrugged. 'All right.'
Ragan began to play his didgeridoo.
Jago kicked at the sand. 'Dawu is getting another foot.'
Yukuwa looked up. 'What do you mean?'
'It's true. Gali is working on it now.'
Yukuwa stared at Jago. 'He is a galka – a sorcerer?'
Jago laughed. 'No, but sometimes he is clever ...'
But it was Gali who had served a meal to the spirits of the sea on the first day. Not Tale, the holy man.
'Come and see,' Jago said.
Yukuwa hunched his shoulders and looked at Ragan.
Ragan looked away. 'Maybe later. We've got to finish this song.'
'Yes, later.' Yukuwa said. We don't want magic here, in Old People's Camp. But it is Dawu. 'No, I'll come.'
Yukuwa followed Jago with a troubled backward glance at Ragan.
A new foot was magic, very big magic. One-Eye could make Gathul break his arm, he could make a snake bite Wapiti, he could make a man die. But One-Eye could not make a new foot.
Yet Gali could. Smiling Gali, the sorcerer.
Yukuwa stepped past Madya, sitting on a tuft of grass with a pipe in his mouth but with his eyes closed.
One-Eye was a galka, from his shuffling walk to his cold voice to his glittering stare. But Gali laughed and sang. How could he be a sorcerer?
Jago led Yukuwa towards the house for trepang – now the smokehouse. The bamboo framework was covered in a grass and pandanus roof. The house was as big as a hill, but from end to end it seeped smoke.
'Where is Dawu?' said Yukuwa, and he stopped.
Jago lifted a heavy curtain in the wall. 'In here.'
Yukuwa stood outside for a long moment, then he

stepped into the smoke. He coughed, panted hot air and blinked stinging eyes as he groped through the swirling shadows. There was a bamboo platform at chest height, crowded with slowly drying trepang. Yukuwa stumbled against a ladder leaning on the platform and began to climb.

'No, down here.' Jago had moved under the platform.

Yukuwa stepped from the ladder and ducked after Jago. He could feel the heat increase with every step, sweat rolling down his body, his legs scorching. He was moving between trenches filled with coals. The smoke-house was a huge ground oven, slowly cooking him.

'There,' said Jago, and pointed.

Yukuwa saw figures caught in the glow of the coals deep in the smokehouse. He stepped slowly until he recognised Dawu, gleaming with sweat and with his mouth open, as if he was about to laugh.

Gali was squatting ahead of him, playing with the coals so they flared across his face and shone in his eyes. He pulled something glowing red from the coal-bed *with his hand*. He placed it on a shining block, and tapped it lightly with a black club.

'Soon,' said Gali, and flashed his teeth at Yukuwa. He squared himself, raised the club above his head and struck.

A thunderclap!

Worse than ten thunderclaps, worse than the Lightning Serpent splitting a tree! Yukuwa heard the sound, his teeth heard it, his bones heard it ...

Yukuwa tumbled from the smokehouse and ran. He bolted down the hill, over the sun-dried trepangs, through the circle of gutting women, and along the beach. He clawed at the air as he passed the shelters, the oyster cliffs and wheezed towards Madya on his tuft of grass.

The pipe drooped from Madya's mouth and fell.

Instinctively he bent forward to pick it up.

And collided with Yukuwa's pumping legs, spinning across the sand as Yukuwa sprawled. They both sprang to their feet, but the kris was in Madya's hand before he realised what had happened.

'You! You again!' Madya sliced the air.

Yukuwa pointed at the smokehouse as he danced back. 'Gali ...'

'Gali. The bloody Bugis! He sends you to attack me ...'

'What's wrong?' Ragan was walking up behind Madya, carrying the didgeridoo.

Madya turned and skipped backwards quickly towards the water. 'Come on, come on, the pair of you! I can take ten of you.' He waved the kris.

'I didn't mean to hit you,' Yukuwa said shakily.

'You didn't mean ... ' Madya breathed heavily, switching his eyes between the boys. He grunted in disgust and sheathed his kris, but he pointed at Yukuwa. 'You can keep, Monkey.' He walked away.

Ragan shrugged. 'Crazy man. What was that sound?'

Yukuwa felt a slight shudder at the base of his spine. 'Galka,' he said. Madya had been forgotten.

'What is he doing to Dawu?'

Yukuwa stared at the smokehouse for a while, then he took a slow and unsteady step.

'Where are you going?'

'Got to go back.'

As he walked alone past the oyster cliffs he heard the terrible sound several times. Distant, but it quivered in his body. He moved slowly past the casuarina trees and the shelters of the tribe. The sound stopped, but every tingling nerve was waiting for it to start again.

Jago was waiting for him, sitting on a stump like a lizard in the sun. 'What happened, big hunter?'

'Where's Dawu?'

'In the smokehouse.'

'Still there? With Gali?'

'Yes. Why, what's wrong?'

'I've got to get him out ...' Yukuwa lurched towards the curtain.

The curtain lifted and Dawu walked out.

Just like that, left foot, right foot. As if the shark had been a bad dream. Yukuwa wanted to spin on the balls of his feet and run again. This was magic, and he could not understand it.

Yet here was Dawu beaming at him, holding his hands wide, inviting him to come up and touch. To see that he was as real as the gravel under his toes.

Impossible.

'How do you like it?' said Dawu, taking a step. 'Isn't Gali a fine marrnggitj?'

Marrnggitj? The healer. The spirits come and offer some people the gift of magic. 'Which one?' they say. 'Galka or Marrnggitj? To kill or to heal? You must choose, you cannot do both.' So One-Eye was a galka and Gali the Macassan is a marrnggitj.

Yukuwa smiled at Dawu and stepped forward.

Dawu was different. Oh yes, there were changes and he should have noticed those before. Dawu was wearing those strange cylinders of material some of the Macassans walked around in – those 'trousers'. He had a foot sticking out of the left cylinder of those trousers, but it was different to any other foot Yukuwa had ever seen. It was short, it was almost round and it was – yes – it was mangrove wood.

'I will dance with this.' Dawu shifted and his face flickered.

Gali staggered though the curtain with something black, heavy and gleaming in his arms. It looked like a crocodile's snout rammed in a block of wood, but it was far too heavy for wood. He put the thing on the ground, rubbed the back of his ear with an odd club and looked smugly at Dawu's mangrove foot. 'Good?'

'Ah ...'

Dawu took two little steps, winced, flapped his arms for a moment, then steadied. He pointed at Yukuwa. 'You ran!'

Yukuwa wanted to run again.

'It's all right,' Dawu said.

Gali offered his club to Yukuwa with a smile. He was wearing a second skin on his hands, something like blackened leather, and he carried strange tools in his belt.

Yukuwa reached for the club and felt the weight of its head.

'Iron,' said Dawu. 'Like the spearheads and nails we get from the Macassans. And this.' He lifted his trouser leg. The mangrove foot had a ring of shining metal with four long metal fingers connecting the ring to a padded ring around Dawu's leg.

This Yukuwa could understand. He hefted the club vaguely.

'Now you hit this with that.' Dawu pointed at the anvil.

Yukuwa shifted his eyes to Gali but Gali only smiled. Timidly, he tapped the anvil and caused a dull clang.

'Hit it!'

Yukuwa swung hard at the anvil and it clapped like stormclouds clashing together. The ringing stayed in the air long after the impact. The sound was terrible, but this time *he* had made it.

'Iron on iron,' Dawu said. 'Just a new sound. A new foot, a new boat ... A new boat.' He nudged Gali, almost playfully. 'Let's go for a walk.'

Yukuwa frowned as he watched Gali walk Dawu and his new foot carefully down to the beach.

Come on, you're happy, really happy, that the old grouch can walk again, right? Yes, yes, don't mind this odd empty feeling.

As if you have lost something …

9 THE CHANGING

Things change, Yukuwa thought. Here is a pile of new-season figs and nuts brought by Duyga for the Macassans to mix with their rice, and here is Laba, the captain, nibbling the nuts and actually losing an argument to Duyga. About planting things like tamarind trees and rice. And there is Gali strumming his coconut, his fire trenches dead behind him, and Madya paddling a canoe filled with the empty boiling dishes back to the boat.

And here is Dawu, the old grouch, grinning.

'You want something,' muttered Laba to Dawu, still watching Duyga walking away. 'I can tell.'

Gali stopped strumming. 'There's little work to be done now, boss.'

'Hardly anything,' said Dawu and winked at Yukuwa.

Yukuwa smiled back. Two moons ago Dawu was shuddering with the pain of that mangrove foot. As if the mangrove foot was the shark and wouldn't let go. He had toppled so many times that children played Falling Dawu in the shallows. But yesterday, when the last of the trepang were laid in the smokehouse, he was dancing on the beach. Oh, in the evenings he still seemed alone, with the Wata families babbling around him, but now he was ready to laugh.

'Well, what is it?' said Laba.

'We want to take a canoe out,' said Dawu.

Yukuwa looked away. 'We' now meant Dawu and Gali, not Dawu and Yukuwa.

'Fine, go. Take Jago's canoe.'

Jago sat up and punched Yukuwa on the shoulder. 'We should go, too. So I can show Yukuwa how the sail works.'

'Get out of here!'

In the end, two canoes and six people left Old People's Camp. Bawi and Ragan wanted to come too so Gali took out the second canoe, leaving Jago in charge of the first, with Yukuwa and Dawu. Yukuwa occasionally and deliberately splashed him while Dawu studied everything.

Jago raised the mast in his canoe and unrolled the matting of the sail. The canoe slid past the massive Macassan boat, now as familiar as an outcrop of rock, leaving behind Bawi and Ragan wrestling with Gali's sail.

Dawu put his paddle beside him. 'This is better. Very much better.'

Yukuwa looked back at distant Gali. Much better.

But Dawu was running his hands over the hull, measuring its thumbnail thickness, feeling the smooth curve of the outside, touching the rough marks made by a tool on the inside.

'It is cut from the trunk of a tree,' Jago said.

'Yes, from a tree like we have here. How is it cut?'

Jago shrugged. 'People on a little island make them for us.'

'So you don't know how they are made.'

'I know. Of course I know. There's a man at home makes everything, from a canoe to our big boat.'

Dawu nodded.

The canoes sailed across a wide bay and into a narrow inlet. The breeze pushed them along a slowly narrowing channel, with only an occasional paddle stroke to correct the course.

'You could sleep here,' said Dawu, and sprawled.

But the sails had to come down when the waterway twisted, and the canoes stopped dead when the mangrove roots caught the outriggers.

'These are no good,' Bawi slapped his canoe's outrigger. 'Bark canoes are better.'

Dawu looked at the winding water ahead and the network of roots caging the carved logs and the poles of the canoes. 'We take them off.'

'You can't do that,' Jago said. 'The canoes will fall over.'

But Dawu cut the knots and cast the outrigger from Jago's canoe. He shimmied the canoe in the water and wobbled an eyebrow at Jago. He hung the outrigger on a branch as they paddled off into the mangroves.

They pushed the canoes across a stretch of flood plain and stepped out into the shallow water, looking for eggs or birds. Bawi speared a goose and walked towards Yukuwa, waving the bird over his head.

Yukuwa saw ripples arrowing towards Bawi's back.

'Feast! We'll have a feast tonight!' shouted Bawi.

The line of low bumps, the hooded eyes ...

Yukuwa jerked his spear up. 'Bawi!'

'Now find the eggs, eh?' Bawi was grinning at him.

The long mouth opening ...

Yukuwa hurled the spear.

'Hey!'

The spear hit the head, glissaded across the ridged back and thumped into a log. Bawi turned, saw the mouth and made a hopeless effort to leap away. Another spear hissed past Yukuwa's flung arm to plunge down the crocodile's throat. The crocodile stopped, shook the spear like a pup with a stick, then slammed the mouth shut to splinter it. Bawi snatched up Yukuwa's spear, killing the crocodile with a thrust into its eye.

From a distance Gali shouted: 'Good hunting!' Jago clapped.

'Ho!' But Bawi muttered to Yukuwa: 'You're so bad a hunter you're dangerous to be with. I won't hunt with you again.' He moved away.

Dawu heard this. 'That from the hunter who threw a spear at a kangaroo and hit the Widow's husband! Don't worry about it.'

But Yukuwa knew Bawi was right.

The rains stopped. A breeze wafted from the east one afternoon, and stayed to sweep the last tumble of grey cloud from the sky.

Laba sniffed the air. 'Time we went home.'

Gathul nodded. 'First we celebrate. A feast, a corroboree.'

Ragan played the didgeridoo, Gathul sang, Duyga and the women danced of the brolgas mating. Yukuwa clicked the clapping sticks, but mechanically. His heart wasn't in it.

The Macassans brought more rice, tea, cloth, iron and a few bottles from their camp, as presents and as payment for the long work.

Jago placed a bright red sarong on Yukuwa's knees with a grin. 'For a great hunter.'

Yukuwa winced. 'Not funny.'

'Not being funny. This is from Laba. I told him about you and the crocodile.'

Yukuwa looked at Jago's face and realised that this time he was serious. 'You told him *what*?'

'Standing up to that monster. Madya would have run all the way home to Macassar.'

'There was no ...'

'And that throw! Straight down the throat! It wasn't Bawi's crocodile, it was yours. Great, great!'

'My throw?' He looked up from the sarong, but Jago

was already running down the beach.

Yukuwa sat on the sand and shook his head. What happened? What did he see? Jago was a hundred paces back. He might see you throw a spear and then see Ragan's spear hit the crocodile. He might think he had seen one spear – he might not have seen Ragan throw his spear at all.

Yukuwa sighed and began to search for Jago. Laba saw him, smiled and started to say something, but Dawu caught Laba by the elbow.

'I want to learn how to make the canoes,' said Dawu.

'You like our canoes?' said Laba. 'Then they are yours. We get more when we come back.'

Jago and other Macassans capered across the beach to Gali's strumming.

Dawu tapped his wooden foot. 'I would still like to learn.'

Ragan leapt to his feet and danced a one-legged hunter. He was greeted with rolls of laughter.

'All right, Dawu, come with us!'

Bawi danced of a hunter who couldn't throw a spear. Yukuwa watched him with a dead face, then returned to his clapping sticks.

After the dancing had finished, when Macassans and the Yolngu were laughing and wrestling in the water, Yukuwa saw Dawu talking to Duyga.

She shook her head violently and turned away. Dawu tried again and she listened to him with her face like stone. When he finished she stood there, refusing to say anything to him. As he walked from her she lifted her head with her eyes wet.

Dawu thumped over to Yukuwa and squeezed his shoulder. 'You're going to be a great hunter. Greater than Bawi, better than Ragan.'

Yukuwa smiled with a little pain. 'No,' he said.

'We are going to Macassar.'

Part Two

10 THE MONEY BOX

Yukuwa stood on the deck of the boat and shivered to the cold wail floating across the water.

You should not be here.

The sarong trapped his legs, his toes touched rattan instead of sand, he smelled dried trepang, tamarind and bitter spices and everything around him creaked, flapped and rocked. The boat was coming to life again, hauling the Macassans back to sunset – taking him with them.

He stared at the women swaying on the sand. Duyga, Wapiti – all his mothers – were crying for him.

You want to cry, too. Oh, last night it was all right. Last night you were with the Moon, the Sisters and the legends. Duyga was weeping, but Dawu gave you the sea and the stars. That was last night. Now the great adventure has curled into a dilly bag of lizards' tails. You can't spear a fish, you are frightened of a dead galka, you need to have Duyga, Gathul, the whole Wata tribe around you. Ragan should be on this boat, not you ...

Men were yelling at each other around Yukuwa as a sail unrolled at the bow. Above him another sail unfolded – a long one, and the boat, the *Gaddong* – the Money Box – began to move out of the bay.

You could jump. You could rip off the sarong, dive from the *Gaddong* and swim back to the tribe.

Dawu clapped his hand on Yukuwa's shoulder. 'Now the journey begins. You'll never forget this.'

But Yukuwa was looking at Dawu's purple sarong, kris and the folded cloth on his head. Dawu was becoming a stranger, leaving him alone.

Gali shouted at the men at the bow and they hauled up the anchors, wooden crosses weighted with heavy stone.

'Bit scary, isn't it?' Jago had been watching him.

'What?' Yukuwa turned from Dawu.

'When you leave. Just now.'

Yukuwa blinked at Jago in surprise. *He* has done this. The crazy boy with the big knife had gone through all this at the other end.

He nodded heavily.

'It gets better. Grab a rope and pull.'

Yukuwa left Dawu alone and helped Jago haul the mainsail to the top of the tripod mast. The sky was blotted out by the sails as the edge of the *Gaddong* dipped to the creaming sea.

'It's a sweet wind,' said Laba. 'We'll be home in a month.'

Yukuwa clung to one of the mast poles and looked back at the distant Old People's Camp, but he could not see the women now. He looked at the Macassans around him, men standing upright with legs cocked for the slanted deck, as if they had been born on the boat, had lived all their lives under the huge seagull wings. The tribe was gone and it was too late to do anything.

'Monkey ...'

Madya squatted on the matting roof and leered down at him.

'Leave him alone, Madya,' Jago said quickly.

'Doing nothing, Captain's Monkey.'

Jago glared at him.

'Just asking Monkey if he likes the sea. It's a long voyage ...'

'You watch for his spear.'

'I'm not a sleepy crocodile. *You* watch.' Madya moved away.

Yukuwa turned to Jago. 'Look, that crocodile ...'

'Ah, don't worry about him.'

Yukuwa sighed. The crocodile didn't matter. It didn't matter at all.

Yukuwa stood high on the stern as the *Gaddong* slid along the coast, and he began to settle down.

All right, there's nothing to worry about here. You can work it all out. Look over the sides and there's two rudders steering the boat like paddles. Right? The sails up there – the great seagull wings – are only matting, like the sail on Jago's canoe and the deck cover you're standing on. And under that is where the crew sleeps. Before the mast is Laba's small shelter and tiny shelters for some noisy birds. Everything makes sense. The *Gaddong* is Old People's Camp, with its shelters, fire and things to eat. The only difference is that the *Gaddong* moves.

'When do we eat them?' Yukuwa pointed at the birds.

'What, the cocks?' Jago seemed shocked. 'We *never* eat them.'

'Oh.' Yukuwa was disappointed. He had heard them often from the beach, crowing just before dawn, and wondered how they would taste. 'Very big birds. One bird could maybe feed four people.'

'Don't even think about it. They are far more important than you.'

'Magic birds?'

'They are our navigators.'

'They tell you where to go?'

'They smell reefs and tell us before we hit them.'

Dawu called Yukuwa over and pointed at the distant coast. 'Beach of Trees already, and the sun is still high. So fast.'

'Yes.' Yukuwa felt flat. He could see only a white sliver of sand and the dark green of the trees. He was too far out to see the shelters.

Dawu glared at Kingfish Beach, as if he was hunting the shark.

'It's a big place, your land.' Jago was cleaning his kris with lemon.

'Yes. I suppose.' Yukuwa said.

'All Yolngu land?'

'Ah, no. There are many different peoples. Djinba, Gunavidji, Burara ... just around here.'

'Do you fight?'

'Fight?' Yukuwa looked back at the Beach of Trees. 'Sometimes.'

'We fight. On my island there are Macassans and Bugis and we fight great battles. Gali is not a Macassan. He is a Bugis.'

Yukuwa remembered Madya calling him that after the fall from the smokehouse roof. He'd made 'Bugis' sound like a slug. 'And you fight?'

'Used to fight.' Jago sounded disappointed. 'But we still fight pirates.'

'Pirates?'

'Boats like ours – and they attack any time. I am getting ready.' Jago flashed his kris.

'I should get my spears ready?'

Jago looked up and saw Yukuwa's face. 'Hey, don't worry.'

He beckoned Yukuwa to the bow, to a box near the

anchors. He opened the box to show a cylinder of metal, stained with salt.

'An anvil,' said Yukuwa wisely.

'No! It is something we stole from the Balandas.' Jago saw the blank look on Yukuwa's face. 'Big, fat, hair all over their faces and grey skins, like trepang before the mangrove dye.'

'Demons,' said Yukuwa bleakly.

'Madya wants to fight them all the time. But we don't fight Balandas, we just steal their cannon.'

'Cannon? That's what this is?'

'Yes. Isn't it great?'

It looked like a log that had been smouldering for a long time.

'What does it do?'

'It kills people. It kills many people. It's for the pirates.'

'How?'

'See that black hole? You point it at the pirates and it roars and the pirates fall dead.'

Yukuwa edged away. 'You see it do that?'

Jago hesitated. 'Gali told me.'

In the late afternoon Yukuwa saw the sacred mountain of Nhulunbuy slide past, no more than a hill sitting on the water. There would be the camp of the Barra tribe and Wanduwa, but Dawu wasn't looking. He was talking lazily with Laba at the stern.

Laba pointed it out. 'That's your last landmark. To get to Old People's Camp we come from the west, along the long Marege coast. But to go home we sail north, with the wind behind us. Into the empty sea.'

Yukuwa stopped listening. His initial fears were dying now, to be replaced by an empty despair. He felt he was carrying a great hole in his stomach.

The long bamboo yards were now an extension of the

mast, with the great sails standing on end, reaching for the clouds. He watched all the winds in the sky tumbling against the sails, scudding the *Gaddong* away from his land.

He remembered the argument Laba had lost. Duyga, smiling at Laba with his planted seeds, marking land which was *his*. 'No,' she said. 'We don't own land. The land owns us.'

You are slipping away from the land, from your waterhole and totem, from the whirling birds and the ticking bush. From the songs and the dances, from the ceremonies that mark every step in your life. You are slipping away, as if you have never existed.

Nhulunbuy caught the last glimmer of the sun, then it had gone.

11 EMPTY SEA

The first night was very bad. Yukuwa tried to sleep down below in the crew's cabin, but he felt trapped in a black box, full of strange sounds and smells. He could hear the sea hissing at his ear, the hull creaking, giving way ... He moved up on deck and tried to sleep between the snoring lumps of Dawu and Laba, but the deck moved under him, trying to tip him into the sea. He clung to the matting, stared at the swaying stars and waited for dawn.

But the dawn was worse. A fresh wind buffeted the sea, kicking waves against the *Gaddong*, pushing it sideways, hurling spray across the deck. Dawu clung to the mast in grim silence and Yukuwa felt a great lizard twisting in his stomach. He sat on the matting and numbly watched the sea hiss past.

'Good, good!' yelled Laba at the wind. 'We're flying!'

Yukuwa closed his eyes.

When Gali boiled some rice, yams and fish in the stern, Yukuwa crawled up to the bow to lie down and die. He was surprised that One-Eye could reach him so far from home.

Tale, the holy man, stepped into the *Gaddong*'s last canoe.

We're sinking, Yukuwa thought. Good.

But Tale was only bracing himself against the sides of the canoe while he sang.

Jago wandered up with a fig. 'You should try this.'

'No. Go away.'

'It will help.'

'Go away.'

Jago shrugged, bit into the fig and walked away.

But he came back. 'Laba says you have to work.'

'I am dying. I want to go home.'

'Laba says you have to help me steer the ship.'

'Oohooh …'

'Come on.'

Yukuwa crawled back to the mast.

Laba stopped talking to Dawu and nodded. 'Enough. No crocodiles out here. We don't need hunters. We want seamen. Learn to steer.'

Yukuwa looked at Dawu in appeal, but Dawu shrugged.

Jago led Yukuwa through the narrow slot behind the mast and into the hazy gloom of the crew cabin. The rattan deck covered the dried trepang, Dawu's turtle shell and the water, carried in thick bamboo joints. On the deck were bags of rice, yams, coconuts, dried fish, the long pods of the tamarind fruit and a few crewmen, smoking their pipes. The reek swept over Yukuwa, and one of the smokers was Madya.

'Let's go, come on …' Jago pushed.

Yukuwa reeled the length of the cabin, banging his head on the timber crosspieces. Gali nodded from the cooking fire – oil poured into sand in a pan – at the open stern, but Yukuwa hardly noticed him. Jago pointed at a great hole in the boat's side, with an unmanned tiller pointing out to sea. To grip the tip of the tiller he would have to leave the boat.

'Go on, Monkey.' Madya rose to his feet.

Yukuwa stood on the edge of the hole, straightened

as much as his stomach would allow, and toppled from the *Gaddong*.

Jago shouted.

Yukuwa caught the tiller, with his feet still on the boat. His body sagged towards the racing water below him and a passing wave slapped his stomach.

'Not like that!' yelled Jago.

Yukuwa could not move the tiller or pull himself back. He was helpless, a fly in a web.

'Help him, Madya,' Gali said, rising with a small log from the fire.

Madya stepped sideways from the hole, squatted on the framework that held the rudder and reached for Yukuwa's hands. 'Come on, Monkey, come to papa.' He was almost singing the words.

Yukuwa stared up at the Macassan.

'Come on, boy,' Madya gripped Yukuwa by his wrists. 'Come on!' And he wrenched Yukuwa's hands from the tiller.

He's going to drop me!

Yukuwa tried to twist his hands to seize Madya's wrists, but the grip was too powerful.

'What's up, Madya?' Gali was calling, somewhere over his feet.

'Nothing, Bugis. Just saving the Monkey.' And he let go.

Yukuwa shrieked as the water surged up him.

Madya snatched at his hands, grinning as he began to slip.

'Stop playing,' said Gali.

'Who's playing? I'm rescuing you, aren't I, Monkey? Oh, he's gone ...'

Madya's fingers lifted from Yukuwa's hands. He dropped, his head plunging into the white foam.

But the water fell from him, his body banging against

the side of the *Gaddong*. He looked up at his ankles, held by Gali's long hands. Gali swung him aboard as if he was a big fish.

Madya was shouting at Gali: 'An accident ...'

'You want to tell Dawu that?'

Madya didn't answer.

'You're supposed to steer with your *feet!*' said Jago and pointed at Tale, quiet on the other tiller. He clambered across the beam that held both rudders and braced himself with one foot on the edge of the hole and placed the other foot where Yukuwa had put his hands. 'See?'

Yukuwa sat next to Jago and became his shadow, stretching his foot for the tiller. There was nothing much between him and the racing water but that didn't matter now. He was locked in position and Madya was gone.

'All right, then?' Tale called from the other tiller.

Jago looked at Yukuwa. 'We're ready.'

Tale took his feet off his tiller and Yukuwa felt new pressure.

'Push, push,' said Jago, 'Enough.'

Gali returned to the small log he was carving into a model boat. Tale, the thin, bearded holy man joined him.

'Sorry,' said Jago to Yukuwa.

'About what?'

'Madya. He can't get me because of Laba, but you ... ? I shouldn't have got you involved.'

Yukuwa pictured Madya on the frame of the smoke-house roof and found himself smiling. 'It was a great fall.'

'Yes, wasn't it?' Jago frowned and kicked the tiller. 'Laba shouldn't have made them like this.'

'What's wrong with them?'

'They don't *have* to point out to sea like this. He says they make the *Gaddong* safe. He says if the tiller stays inside the boat the steersman goes to sleep. But this way if he goes to sleep he falls into the sea. So he doesn't fall asleep.'

'But some people fall into the sea anyway.'

Jago looked at Yukuwa, then they both laughed.

Yukuwa saw Gali looking at him.

'You are getting over it,' Gali said.

'I will make a bark painting for you.'

'Don't worry about it. How d'you like my boat?' He held up his model.

'Ah, yes.' So far it looked more a log than a boat. 'This is a toy for your children?'

'It is not a toy,' said Gali, a little peeved.

'Hah!' said Tale. His heavy eyebrows bristled.

'Look at the trepang we got after we gave the sea spirits a feast.'

Tale pointed a warning finger at the sky. 'Do not ask for trouble.'

Gali grunted and crouch-walked to the entrance.

Tale bent towards Yukuwa. 'It's a toy,' he said and shuffled out.

Yukuwa looked at Jago.

'A weapon against the pirate. The cannon is better.'

Yukuwa settled back and concentrated on following Jago's interpretation of Laba's shouted commands.

Jago looked sideways at him. 'See? You get used to it.'

'The boat?'

'Everything. The boat, leaving home.'

Yukuwa thought. 'I am missing the tribe.'

'You have Dawu.'

'Sometimes.'

'I stopped missing my village the first morning. I never miss it now.'

'What about your friends?' asked Yukuwa.

Jago shrugged. 'Push the tiller.'

Yukuwa tried to keep a shadow steady on his knee and after a while Laba cut down on the shouting. Slowly he understood what he was doing. 'We are running the *Gaddong* now. Just the two of us,' he said.

Jago nodded. 'Don't let Laba know.'

Yukuwa pressed the tiller and saw the distant bowsprit slide slowly across the horizon. He eased off, but he now knew he could control this massive boat with his foot. He felt the power in his toe and stopped worrying about the boat, about Madya, the pirates, even the Balanda demons.

And forgot the lizard in his stomach.

Yukuwa slowly grew to understand the boat, but never the sea. The horizon would not change, a distant unbroken flat line that pushed out the sun in the morning and reclaimed it in the evening. Columns of light swept across the water, and birds scratched the sky, but they passed. There was nothing solid to see, nothing to pass, to move towards. Yukuwa felt like an ant on a rock, becoming smaller, smaller, with every passing day.

But the mood was not his alone. One long afternoon Dawu sat with Yukuwa and talked of wallabies, dancing and the tribe, always staring at the sea.

'It's big, isn't it?' Yukuwa finally said.

Dawu stopped. 'So much water. What is the good of a Yolngu here?'

'What's the good of a Macassan here? It must end some time.'

'I think that I will wake up one morning and the Macassans and their boat will have slipped into the depths of the sea. Even Gali.' Dawu was not smiling.

'It's a long way to swim back.'

Dawu looked closely at Yukuwa. 'Are you frightened?'

Yukuwa hesitated. He knew how the *Gaddong* worked

and he had known that crazy Macassan boy for a long while now. 'No. Not any more.'

Dawu nodded slowly and turned to the sea. 'Good,' he said.

A little later Yukuwa watched him limp across to Laba. 'How do you know where you are? Just by the stars?'

'The sea.' Laba nodded. 'I read the sea. The pattern of the waves, the colour of the water, the glow under the surface at night.'

'Oh,' Dawu said and limped away.

And Yukuwa realised that Dawu the hunter was lost – far more lost than he had ever been – on this endless water.

The gentle rhythm of the boat nibbled at the days. Tale would greet the morning with a soft drone, always looking across the sea towards a sacred place called Mecca. Laba would wander about his boat, feeling the taut ropes, adjusting knots, inspecting the sails. Gali would cook a fish stew with tamarind fruit and rice in a fat clay pot and the crew would sit about the boat eating breakfast from clay bowls. Laba would give little jobs to the crew in the morning, weaving new rattan rope, replacing the old rope that ran between the two rudders, stitching sails, repairing woodwork . . .

In the afternoon the crew would have most of the time to themselves. After they had prayed quietly they gathered around Gali and his kecapi.

Close up, the kecapi was a polished coconut shell and some iron strings pulled tightly on a curved piece of wood. To make the kecapi sing, Gali held the shell against the iron strings and plucked them. He used his kecapi to give him a rhythm for making a song, as Ragan had played his didgeridoo for Gathul.

Usually he sang light songs. He sang of two fishermen

who were fierce rivals. The first man came ashore with a fish as big as him and boasted about it for a week. The second man brought back a fish as long as his canoe and he boasted about it for a month. The first man was so angry that he sailed off to Marege, where he looked for the biggest fish in the world. And he caught it …

'Yes?' said Yukuwa.

Gali laughed. 'He is still out there, in the strange waters of Marege. He can't go home because his boat is being towed about by the biggest fish in the world. He can't let go because – after all – he caught it.'

But once Gali sang a grim song, of a fierce king attacking another kingdom with sword and cannon, putting a prince to flight and killing his father and grandfather with cudgels …

Then he saw Madya's face and let the song die.

The crew would doze, stretch in the sun, and watch Gali working on the evening meal. They would eat and Tale would sing as the sun set.

Laba was staring at piled cloud sitting on the horizon.

'Reading the sea?' Yukuwa said.

'Letting the clouds tell him where he is,' said Jago.

'But clouds move around.'

'Not all the time.'

'Heyah!' Laba swept his arm down on the cloud and the *Gaddong* followed.

An hour later a knuckle of land nudged the horizon and Jago was as smug as a crocodile with a duck in its belly. Dawu noticed this as he helped Gali with the breakfast.

The new land rose from the sea like teeth. Yukuwa watched isolated brown points slowly lift from the water and reach for each other. Jagged islands became hills, became mountains far higher than Nhulunbuy. By late afternoon the new land was grinning, showing its fangs and waiting.

'It's Tanimbar,' said Jago.

'Oh,' said Yukuwa. New land, strange land, with different spirits …

'There are cannibals and head-hunters around here, hey Gali?'

Yukuwa stared at the sombre green mountains.

Gali saw Yukuwa's face. 'We never see them. See there?'

A small mountain drifted away from the grinning land, revealing new water, opening a way to another sea.

'That's ours. Head-hunters have their mountains, we have the sea.'

Next day the new land was gone and the *Gaddong* was alone again.

12 MACASSAN WATER

Then there was no wind, and the *Gaddong* sat on a sea as still as polished rock. Nothing to see but the sun crawling across the sky, not even a wandering bird. Yukuwa listened to the mutter of the men, the low creaking of the yards, and sweated and wished he could feel sand between his toes.

Jago sprawled next to Yukuwa at the bowsprit. 'What're you doing?'

Yukuwa was staring at the green water beneath him. 'Thinking.'

'What about?'

'Ragan and me, we used to stay like this for half a day. Time didn't matter. When we were kids, when spears didn't matter that much.'

'What were you doing?'

'We'd stare down frogs.'

Jago laughed. 'Stare at frogs! I'd die of boredom!'

'So what did you do when you were a kid?'

'Battle! We went across the river and fought for the fort. A real fort with bullets and bones still in the grass. We – that's me and Mustari – were Balandas and Macassans, and we fought to the death. Staring at frogs!'

'This Mustari – he is your friend?' Yukuwa was puzzled

by a faint and awkward feeling. As if he were somehow jealous of this Mustari boy.

'When he wasn't a Balanda! Yes, we did everything: fishing, climbing trees, exploring – and battle! We would sit in the sand and think of great things to do, then we would go and do it. We never were with the other kids. They never understood us. They were too dull.'

'Why didn't he come on the *Gaddong*?'

A shadow passed across Jago's face. 'He died last year. Sick of malaria and died.'

Yukuwa and Jago looked at each other.

'Oh,' said Yukuwa.

'Yeah.'

In the afternoon of the second day of stillness, the heat was so intense Gali threw water on the matting so the crew could move around without pain.

And Madya suddenly yelled at Gali: 'Liar!'

Gali put the bucket down.

'Yes, you! Sultan Hasanuddin does not kill with cudgels. Liar!'

'All right. Sorry.' Gali went back to Dawu.

Madya stood on the deck with his fists flexing, trying to find words and failing. He walked away.

Yukuwa remembered the grim tale Gali had sung, but shrugged it aside. He was happy that Madya was angry with Gali instead of him.

The wind returned at midnight.

A cock called in the early morning and Yukuwa saw Laba and Gali stumbling around the dark boat, trying to see what the bird had sensed in the water. Gali pointed at a faint ripple of white off the bow, and the steersman turned the *Gaddong* away from the reef. Gali and Laba went back to sleep.

Yukuwa lay awake on the matting and stared at the dark sea, where only strange birds could see danger. This water was only for Macassans, never for Yolngu. He turned to the watching eyes of Dawu.

A few hours later, Yukuwa saw Dawu frowning at the cocks. 'Something wrong, Dawu?'

Dawu snorted. 'No bird is smarter than me. Nowhere.'

And he finally wandered to the stern, nodding at the line in Gali's hands. 'Fishing?'

'What else? But they don't like me.'

'They are not here. They're over there.'

Yukuwa followed Dawu's outstretched arm to a span of sea. There was nothing there. To his eyes. He slowly began to smile.

Gali squinted. 'There?'

'Yes.'

'I don't see anything.'

'They're there,' said Yukuwa.

Gali frowned. 'Can *you* see anything?'

'No. But he can.' And Yukuwa wanted to shout.

Gali looked at the steersman and lifted his eyebrows. The man eased the tiller back. Laba opened one eye from his doze.

'Just a correction,' said Gali, and Laba closed the eye.

Yukuwa thought he could see something in the water now. Some sort of shadow, as if a small cloud was passing before the sun.

Dawu picked up his harpoon and waited.

'Fish, fish!' Tale shouted from the bow and raced back for a net.

Dawu hurled his harpoon and the cane trap on the end of Gali's line began to bounce about.

Jago was astonished.

Gali was puzzled. 'But this is our water. We should

show you how to catch our fish in our water.'

Dawu shrugged. 'Fish is fish.'

Yukuwa leaned back and grinned, like a crocodile with a wallaby in its belly. Water is water.

Yukuwa was very nervous as the *Gaddong* nudged past the long black shape of an island in the quiet night.

Dawu had suddenly given him his clapping sticks after a sad song from Tale, and said: 'Your turn, now.'

'I'm not a songman,' he said, staring at the sticks.

'Yes, you are.'

He looked sideways to Jago, who waved a handful of fish and rice at him to make him get on with it, at Gali, who was strumming his kecapi, and at the crew, who were grinning at him.

'Or you swim home,' said Jago, looking up from his rice.

Yukuwa looked at the stars hopelessly. You can't just sing a Yolngu song in Yolngu. You have to sing a Yolngu song in Macassan. Different words, different rhythm. Remember working on a song like that with Ragan? An afternoon it took, and it still didn't come out right. This is going to be terrible.

'The Moon Story,' he said, and the sticks in his hands clicked out a rhythm. Gali followed the sticks.

He wobbled into a song of how Moon's children caught fish and a goose but gave nothing to Moon. So Moon made a net and caught the greedy children in it. He threw the greedy children into a waterhole, and that was the end of them.

Some of the crew laughed and pointed at Jago, who was still eating.

Yukuwa began to relax and sang that Moon's wives were so angry at this that they chased him up the tallest tree and threw sticks at him until he had to climb into the sky.

'There he is, Old Moon.' Yukuwa pointed a stick.

The crew laughed and clapped, astonishing Yukuwa.

But Laba stared bleakly at the moon. 'It is too bright,' he said.

The laughter died. Men started to stare out into the night, trying to see something between the shine and the shadow.

'What is it?' Yukuwa felt his warm glow fade.

Gali rubbed his hand against his knee. 'This is pirate water ...'

'No.' Laba was facing the long dark island. 'This is *our* water.'

Gali looked at him, and at the island. 'Maybe it is Dawu's and Yukuwa's, too.'

Laba cocked an eyebrow, then he shrugged. 'It was a beginning ...'

Madya muttered: 'It was an end.'

Gali nodded past Yukuwa. 'It's why we started to come to Marege. That's one of the Buton islands and in the water here the Macassans lost a battle with the Balanda. A few survivors came to Marege, into the great gulf. Laba's great grandfather sailed past Old People's Camp, to a big bay, and the leaders anchored in the shelter of an island.'

Dawu pictured Gali's words. 'Wobalinna Island.'

'And they found trepang ...'

Madya pushed Gali angrily aside. 'That's it? All of it? It's not their water, and never yours, Bugis! It's Macassan water! It's got Macassan blood – '

'All right, Madya.' Laba said tiredly.

'No! The Bugis is making the Battle of Buton sound like a fish fight! You forget ...' He snatched the kecapi from Gali, clawing at the strings, shouting:

A thousand oars flashing in the sun,
An ocean of sails holding the wind,
Cannon sniffed the air ...

A string snapped on the kecapi. Madya threw the kecapi back at Gali's head. 'That's what we were, Bugis. We would have stood against the sailing fortresses of the Balanda, driven them from our water.'

'It's been a long time,' said Gali.

'Doesn't matter, Bugis. Your prince and his fleet sailed with the Balanda and betrayed us and all the islands. We won't forget until the last Balanda goes home!' Madya looked at the blank faces about him and stamped away.

Gali looked sadly after him, plucking his damaged kecapi softly, almost whispering a snatch of song.

Walls of cannon roar fire.
Muffling the wind, dimming the sun.

He stopped. 'I know that song. Half of me is Bugis, half of me is Macassan. After fifty years, what difference does it make?'

Dawu peered into the darkness. 'There's a boat out there.'

'Where?' Laba was at his side.

Dawu pointed at the blackness off the bow.

Nothing. Nothing but the winking of a low star and a glimmer on the water.

'No sound.' Laba gestured to Tale on the tiller and the *Gaddong* began to turn from the glimmer. 'Cannon. Softly, now.'

The Macassans moved over the boat, silent shadows. Madya and a handful of men worked the sails, Dawu and Yukuwa gathered their spears from the crew's cabin. Yukuwa's hands were damp. Gali picked up his unfinished model boat, shook his head and replaced it before he moved towards the cannon. Jago drew his kris halfway from the sheath and crouched beside Yukuwa.

Finally Yukuwa saw the shape of the other boat against the stars.

'Have they seen us?' Gali whispered, holding a long piece of iron.

'They aren't turning ...'

'They've seen us.'

The moon slid clear of the cloud. The two boats were no more than a hundred metres apart, each lined with staring men. Nobody moved as the boats drew a little nearer, then slowly apart. They passed each other without a sign or a nod, until the moon slid into a thick black bag and the *Gaddong* was alone again.

'Not a pirate,' said Gali.

'Just a fishing boat,' said Laba.

13 FISH HOUSE

The first sign of the Macassans' home was a house sitting on the water.

Like a smokehouse, thought Yukuwa, but no smoke, and it is far smaller. And there is nothing else on the still brown sea. As if the house is starting on a journey.

'It's a boat,' said Dawu.

'Never,' said Laba.

'It's a house,' said Yukuwa.

'A fish house,' said Jago, with a nod.

'Fish need a house?'

Jago and Laba laughed together.

The *Gaddong* had sailed from the Buton cluster to the massive island of the Macassans, Celebes. In the shadow of the island, Gali had told how it got its name, how a grey stranger asked a Macassan the name of his home-land, while staring in fear at the Macassan's kris. The Macassan thought he was asking the name of his weapon. So Celebes, the Iron Kris, became the island's name.

Yukuwa had watched the mountains disappear into grey cloud as Jago whispered of Toala, the forest people, ghost people, waiting in the mist.

Suddenly a deep metallic clanging came across the water.

'The gongs. They have seen us,' said Laba.

Drums joined the gongs.
'The house on the water?' said Yukuwa.
'Naah,' said Jago. 'The village.'
'You must be glad to be home?'
'I suppose so.' Jago shrugged.
Yukuwa looked beyond the floating house, to the broad brown river flowing slowly into the sea. Where the river met the sea, several small boats nudged the beach, where lights and low fires were appearing in the dusk. Lights were also being lit on the floating house.
'All this for us?' Dawu said.
'Oh yes.' Laba sounded smug. 'We're the first to return.'
'Even the house on the water?'
'Well, no ...'
'That's for the fish,' said Jago quickly. Yukuwa eyed him sharply, but he smiled. 'That's to welcome them to the big party.'
The lights on the house were being lowered to the water.
'Fishing,' said Dawu with a nod.
Jago was annoyed. 'Is the house in the right place for the fish?'
Dawu scratched his beard. 'I don't know.'
Jago wobbled an eyebrow at Yukuwa in quiet triumph. Macassan water was for Macassans once more.
A man stepped out from the house and waved at the *Gaddong*.
Laba waved back, then nodded at Tale. 'All right. That's enough.'
Tale and Gali turned the handle at the end of the lower yard and rolled up the bottom sail for the first time in six weeks. The mainsail was partly rolled, until the wave at the bow of the *Gaddong* died to a ripple. Wood creaked softly, as if the boat was sighing.
'Heya! How did you go?' shouted the man at the house.

'Good, good! So much trepang we swell like a cow with calf. We have fine turtle shell and a little ironwood, and,' Laba slapped Dawu on the shoulder, 'and we have brought a native of Marege. Two natives.'

Yukuwa looked across at Dawu but he was still studying the river.

The man at the house was silent for a while. 'Very black, eh?'

'Over there,' Dawu pointed.

'Ah ... ?'

'The fish. They are shoaling.'

Yukuwa smiled at Jago.

'Oh.' Laba called: 'How are the fish?'

'As always, Laba. They're there or they're not.'

'I mean now, Bisbu. Are they there?'

Bisbu yelled back into the house and the lights wobbled below the house. After a murmur Bisbu called across the still water. 'Only a few have come to the lights. Hardly worth pulling the net up. You want some fish?'

'Dawu, here, is a master fisherman, found fish for us all the way from Tanimbar. He says there's fish over there.'

'The fish come here, not there.' Bisbu sounded annoyed.

'All right, good luck with it.'

'This is our water. Not his.'

'Fish is fish.'

Bisbu looked into the house and Yukuwa saw that the house did not have a floor, just a large square hole opening to the sea below.

'All right,' said Bisbu. 'Just this once.'

As the *Gaddong* nosed past the fish house, men with torches clambered up the poles that held the house above the water. But the house was rocking slightly. The poles were not standing on the bottom but were lashed to bundles of floating bamboo. The men lifted a net from the sea bed, then pulled a rope to move the house across the river mouth.

On the beach, men and women stood waiting with torches and children shouted and splashed in the shallows as the *Gaddong*'s mainsail and jib were put away. Jago moved away from Yukuwa and began waving at someone in the crowd. The *Gaddong* nudged through the children to the beach, and Jago leaped into the water. For a moment the children grinned at Jago, welcoming a returning adventurer, then they looked past him and he barged through them towards the beach. The crew hit the water behind him in a roaring avalanche, chased children, laughed and hugged the grinning women.

Yukuwa felt numbly alone.

And Dawu was not helping. 'Look at that ...' he pointed.

Above the noisy crush there were several boats beached among the palm trees. Some of them were as big as the *Gaddong* and each had its own shelter of dried palm leaves. But there was not much difference between these shelters and the shelters of Old People's Camp.

It was the shapes behind the boats. They were far bigger than the fish house on the water, almost as big as the *Gaddong* and they were made of solid wood with square holes and a roof of thin pieces of wood. They had all the solidity of a boat but they were held in the air by thick poles.

'Houses,' said Dawu uncertainly. 'People houses.'

Someone giggled.

From the *Gaddong* Yukuwa looked down at the crowded ring of children, staring with wide eyes at him and Dawu.

'Hello,' he said.

Two little girls started to giggle and then slammed their hands over their mouths. Larger boys swept them out of sight and stood before them, watching gravely.

'What are they staring at?' said Yukuwa.

Dawu shrugged. 'We're black, they're brown. And they're kids.'

'Dawu!' Laba stood on the beach with an important-looking person, and he was waving.

Yukuwa jumped from the *Gaddong*, splashing some of the grave boys, and almost fell to his knees. For the first time in six weeks he was standing on a patch of sand that did not bob, rock or slide and he found it hard to stand. He held his hand up to help Dawu, but Dawu hopped into the water, balanced on his mangrove foot and strode away.

The man beside Laba was tall, lean and with white tufts of hair riding his ears. His sarong and shirt carried flecks of silver and he was carrying a long kris in an elaborate sheath of gold.

'This is the chief of my village, the Karaeng,' said Laba, straightening his back as he spoke. 'And this is Dawu, elder of the Watu tribe of the Yolngu people in Marege.'

The two men studied each other for a while, then the Karaeng bowed his head slightly. 'Welcome to my village.'

'We are happy to be here.'

'After that long voyage? You must be *very* happy to be here.'

'It wasn't that bad.'

'No?'

'I didn't have to walk here.'

The Karaeng looked at the mangrove foot and he smiled. 'Laba says you wish to learn how we make boats.'

'The canoes.'

'Bisbu will help you when he is not fishing. Perhaps you have already helped him.'

'Perhaps.'

'You are a fisherman.'

'I am a hunter.'

Suddenly a cheer roared from the house on the water.

'You are a great fisherman!' The Karaeng clapped Dawu on the shoulder and walked away, laughing.

Things changed after that. The men – even the men who had been on the *Gaddong* – looked at Dawu with new respect, and the children now stared at Yukuwa as if he was some hero from their firelight stories.

Jago came out of the crowd, caught him by the elbow and presented him to his mother. 'This is Yukuwa. He is my friend.'

But a hero can't be a hero all the time.

'Friend?' the short, flat-faced woman said with a touch of alarm.

'Mother, he won't bite.'

She pulled tight the dark blue coat she wore over her sarong and grunted. 'Come on, there's a meal cooking – will they eat rice?' She shuffled away.

'We eat anything,' Yukuwa said.

She stopped.

'Not *everything*, mother,' said Jago.

'You both speak Macassan? People in Marege speak Macassan?'

'We speak Yolngu,' said Yukuwa. 'But we learned a little Macassan from the boat.'

'Yes, you speak odd Macassan.' She snorted and walked off.

Laba followed her with his hand on Dawu's shoulder as he talked. Yukuwa hesitated, but Jago grinned at him and towed him after them, through the crowd. They passed beating drums and gongs and blazing fires on the beach.

Yukuwa saw some of the crew of the *Gaddong* round the fires, no longer with each other but surrounded by their families. Gali waved at him while two small children crawled over him and a young woman ran a finger down his nose. Madya held a slim woman to him as he laughed …

A woman with haunted eyes.

14 THE VILLAGE

Yukuwa woke to the dry smell of rice husks and chicken feathers. The deck was not moving. He opened his eyes when he realised he could feel earth under his fingers.

Morning light was filtering through quivering leaves, but the sky was blocked from him by black wood pillars and a huge roof.

You are in a great fish trap!

He sat up.

No, no, under the house. Off the *Gaddong*, in Celebes – the Iron Kris – and under Jago's house. Under the house, not *in* it, because Jago's mother still thinks you are going to sneak up and eat her.

He clicked his teeth together and smiled at the house above him.

Funny things in that house. Last night you walked on swept wood, sat on chairs and ate rice and chicken on plates from China, at a table. The chicken was the same sort of bird as the navigator bird on the *Gaddong* but here they didn't seem so important. It was cooked in a big metal pot on a fire. The fire was lit on blackened stones so it didn't burn through the wooden floor. You drank water that was taken from a clay pot, so big you could hide in it. Jago sleeps on a bed, even softer than the sand of Old People's Camp.

'Awake at last.' Jago was on the bottom step with two steaming bowls.

Yukuwa reached out to shake Dawu.

'He's gone, hours ago.' Jago passed to Yukuwa a bowl of rice soup with green vegetables and an egg. 'Bisbu came round before dawn to take him out with the fishing fleet. He'll bring him back to Boatbuilders' Beach.'

'Why didn't he wake me?'

'Can you find fish?'

'Well ...'

'You slept like a dead buffalo. We'll go to Boatbuilders' Beach after breakfast.'

Yukuwa looked around him as he ate. There are funny things down here, too. Like a bamboo fence going around a few bags of rice, and some strange tools. And hens and chickens pecking outside the fence. Oh, yes, the fence is to keep the birds off the rice. Simple. And this large white animal with pointed bones on its head staring at you ...

'Don't mind it,' said Jago. 'It's the family goat.'

Yukuwa growled at the family goat and it shuffled backwards. 'Lika a camp dingo?'

'It's more useful than a dingo.'

Jago's mother came down with a small bucket, squinted at Yukuwa and chased the goat. The goat was hampered by a short length of bamboo worn at its neck, making it easy to catch. She began to milk the goat.

'It's more stupid than a dingo,' said Yukuwa.

After she had finished with the goat, Jago's mother cut down some plants growing around the house. Jago said she had planted them herself.

Yukuwa remembered the old argument on the beach. Laba asked Duyga why she didn't plant seeds, make a piece of land her own. Duyga laughed and said the Yolngu didn't own land, the land owned them. Laba said if she planted seeds she would have food at her fingertips. Duyga showed him a gathering dish full of figs and nuts. She said over there was matchbox bean, black fruit, and soon there'd be tubers, bulbs in the flood plains, water-lilies in the pools, yams on the slope and fruit, berries, cycad nuts everywhere. Why plant? The land gives food. It is waiting to be picked up. Laba ate Duyga's figs and shut up.

'What are you grinning about?' Jago said.

'Nothing, nothing at all.'

After the meal Jago led Yukuwa through the village and the village was stranger than Jago's house. They wandered down narrow tracks lined with pebbles and between houses surrounded with sticks to keep the goats out. A little girl passed them in a box on round pieces of wood, pulled by a bad-tempered goat. Later a large animal, much bigger than a kangaroo, trotted down a track with a man on its back. Some boys, spinning a carved piece of wood on the ground, invited Jago to join them. But Jago shook his head with his thumb on his kris and led Yukuwa away. He called the boys 'kids', although they seemed as old as him.

They walked through the middle of the village and a woman brushed past, in tears and with a swollen cheek.

Yukuwa thought she looked like Madya's wife.

Outside the village, women were planting grass in a shallow pond.

'Rice,' Jago said.

Further away a huge animal with flat curving horns dragged a long piece of wood and a man across the pond.

'Buffalo,' Jago said.

Near the pond a man was swinging a very large hammer at a piece of red-hot metal. The ringing sound echoed Gali in the smokehouse at Old People's Camp.

Another man was sitting on a high chair, pumping two long poles in vertical pipes. With every lunge, fire roared out of the ground and a singed third man worked with something in the fire.

'The village furnace,' Jago said. 'They make parts for the boats, ploughs. They once made cannonballs for the fort.'

'Fort? The place where you and Mustari used to go?'

Jago smiled, but with a touch of sadness. 'It was a good time.'

They stopped outside the house of the Karaeng, a vast wooden structure among the treetops. Longer than two *Gaddongs*, it could have slept nearly all the Yolngu people. A carved crest rose at the peak of the roof, a strange bird leaping at the sky.

'See there ... under the carving,' Jago pointed at the front of the house, between the slopes of the roof. The triangle of wood was divided into four horizontal sections. 'That shows the importance of our Karaeng. If he had *five* sections he would be a king, with four he is almost a king. Our house has two sections, so I am related to the king. I told you.'

'Yes, all right.' Yukuwa gave up trying to make sense of the village.

'What's wrong with you? You look as dumb as our goat.'

'How can you move?'

'Move?'

'All the goats, chickens, ducks, the boats that have their own shelters, the rice plants in the pool, the furnace and these huge houses. How can you move on when the land gets tired?'

Jago looked at Yukuwa as if he was talking Yolngu.

'No, no.' Yukuwa suddenly prodded Jago. 'There are *two* villages, right? Maybe three. You plant the rice and go to the second village to live in the houses there, and then you go and live in the third village. Then you come back here and the rice is ready to be picked. Right?'

Jago shook his head.

'No, it can't be that, can it? You would have to build three houses instead of one, far too much work. You leave here for a beach camp, like Old People's Camp. That is easy.'

'No. We never leave.'

'*Never*? You just stay here with the same trees and the same beach, all your lives? It is a good beach and good houses, but it must be dull.'

Jago raised a defensive finger, then nodded. 'Without Mustari ...' he shrugged.

Yukuwa trailed Jago in silence.

Jago suddenly batted at the air. 'Forget it, forget it. It's just dull.'

'I think ...' Yukuwa picked his words. 'You are like us.'

'How?'

'We move all the time. We move when we get tired of a place or the place gets tired of us.'

'Yes. We don't.'

'But you *do* move! You have houses and chickens and goats and furnaces, but when you get tired of that you catch the wind and sail your boats to Marege. You are like us.'

When Jago and Yukuwa reached Boatbuilders' Beach, two men were using mallets to knock an old boat to pieces. But everywhere else boats were being put together. Bisbu was talking to Dawu beside a massive keel, made from three sections of a tree trunk. The keel carried short ribs, making it look like the skeleton of a giant fish.

Bisbu beamed at Yukuwa. 'Good morning, boy. You're late. Your uncle found some fish again.'

'Always,' Yukuwa said with a smile.

Men were now hammering thick planks onto the ribs.

Bisbu stepped away from the din and held up a white cloth. 'I was telling Dawu that I wear this to keep out devils when I finish the keel. But he must know all this.'

Dawu looked tired. 'Some of the fishermen think I'm a dukun. That's a Macassan magic man like One-Eye. No, not like One-Eye.'

Yukuwa smiled. He understood the fishermen. 'Well, maybe ...'

'You shut up.'

'You like my business?' said Bisbu.

Near Bisbu, a man was shaving the face of a plank with an axe, and another plank was being smoothed with something like an axe, except the blade was turned sideways. An adze, Jago said. Both men struck their planks with such precision that the wood was left smooth.

'You'll have to do that when you make your canoe,' Bisbu said.

Further along the beach there were other boats which were more complete. One boat looked like a stone fish, with thousands of needles in its round hull. Each needle was a wooden peg.

Jago picked up a covered bowl and presented it to Yukuwa with a sly smile. 'Feel like some lunch?'

Yukuwa saw the smile and stepped backwards.

Jago whipped the cloth cover off. The bowl was alive with spiders.

'Don't play games with that!' Bisbu snatched the cloth from Jago and replaced it. 'It would take days to get more.'

Jago ducked his head and put the bowl back.

'You understand the spiders?' Bisbu asked Dawu.

'For the magic man?'

'Yes, of course. They are for the caulking ceremony. After the mangrove nails have been driven in we must put a mixture of sap and bark between the planks. The caulking is important because if water comes in, the boat will sink.'

Dawu winced, as if he was remembering the bark canoes.

'So the mixture is important and the ceremony is too. See, there is not a single pebble under the boat, because that would mean that the boat will run onto rocks.

'We use spiders and their webs, so if a sailor rests in the shadow of the boat he will be attracted to her, and will stay.'

Dawu looked at Yukuwa and they slowly smiled together.

'That is funny?'

Dawu shook his head. 'Your spirits are like ours.'

Bisbu grunted and strode back along the beach. 'Enough of big boats, Dawu. It's time you started work on your canoe.'

'You going across the river?' Jago asked.

'Yes, why?'

'We are coming too.' Jago said.

'This is work.'

'We'll work.'

'Hah!'

They walked along the beach to the sheltered boats of the village, Bisbu shouldering an axe and talking about the technique of finding a canoe in a tree, Jago talking about his fortress across the river.

Shouts exploded from the pebbled tracks, stopping Bisbu in mid-stride, stilling fishermen at their dry nets, collapsing the play of children in the sand.

Madya's wife stumbled backwards onto the beach, shouting and staring into the village. Dawu caught the woman as she reeled into him, but she did not seem to be aware of him.

'Stoppit! Stoppit!' she was shrieking.

Two men tumbled onto the sand after her, one holding a flashing kris. Their shouting was replaced by a desperate panting.

'Please ...' Madya's wife turned to Bisbu, her swollen cheek shining. 'They'll kill each other!'

The tumble reached Bisbu and he snatched the kris from Madya. Fishermen pulled the fighting men apart and held them.

'Woman beater!' Gali, the sleepy singer, the peace-maker, tried to kick Madya.

'Bugis bastard!' Madya shouted.

The shouting stopped when the Karaeng strode among the fishermen. He looked at the swelling on the side of the face of Madya's wife, at the kris in Bisbu's hand and at the anger in the faces of Madya and Gali.

'It will not stop, will it?'

'They are not Macassans, her and him,' snarled Madya. 'They are Bugis, men of Bone. They should live with the Balandas.'

'Enough.' The Karaeng looked at his feet for a moment. 'Tomorrow we were going to celebrate the *Gaddong*'s return, eh? With dancing and music. All right, we are still going to do that. But now there is something else – the Dance of the Kris.'

The fishermen released the fighters. Gali and Madya bowed their heads stiffly before the Karaeng and moved away, their eyes fixed.

15 FORTRESS

Bisbu resumed his walk along the beach with Dawu as if nothing had happened. When they reached the bank of the Jeneberang River he touched an old canoe with his foot. 'You want to make something like this?'

It wasn't quite as good as the ones that were unloaded at the Old People's Beach, but the design was the same.

'Yes,' said Dawu.

'Then we'll work from the beginning.'

They pushed the canoe into the water, Bisbu allowing Yukuwa and Jago to paddle across the river.

'They're going to fight,' Jago said, halfway across the river.

'Pity,' Bisbu said heavily. 'Farida was different when the Mad Macassan was not here.'

'Gali is a good-looking man,' said Dawu sadly.

Like Wanduwa's hairy boy, thought Yukuwa.

'Eh? What has that got to do with it?'

'Isn't that it? She doesn't want Madya. She wants Gali.'

Like Wanduwa.

'Farida is Gali's sister.'

'Ah.'

'Bugis,' said Yukuwa.

Bisbu looked at him in surprise. 'Yes, Bugis, and that's all of it. Fifty years ago the Macassans fought the Bugis.

We invaded them, they invaded us. Fifty years ago! In the village this old fighting has been forgotten. When a Macassan fisherman married a Bugis girl, it didn't matter. When they died of malaria their children – Gali and Farida – were Macassan. As it should be.'

'But it hasn't worked out,' Dawu said.

'It is only Madya. Mad Madya. And that is recent. There was nothing wrong in the beginning. Madya married Farida and strutted around the village like a rooster. Then he meets some men in a Macassar bar. He comes home and shouts that Farida is Bugis, was never Macassan, and the war is still being fought.'

'So Madya is going to fight Gali,' Jago said softly.

The canoe touched the gravel. Jago stepped ashore and pulled it after him. Bisbu walked across a clearing and into a young forest until he was surrounded by trees, tall but slim.

'You have to *see* your canoe in the trunk.'

'Like I see the fish,' Dawu said.

'That's it. You look around and find a canoe in the trunk waiting for you to release it.'

Dawu searched for his tree with Bisbu walking behind him.

'No, no, too fat for a canoe, no, see the twist in the wood, no, still too much work for the axe. The tree trunk should be perfect for the skin of the canoe. Yes, that will do. You will improve as you learn. Have you trees like this in Marege?'

Yukuwa thought so, only the bark was different.

When Bisbu began to chop at the tree Jago beckoned Yukuwa away.

'I should stay and help ...'

'They'll be working for hours. Come on, have a look at my fortress.'

Yukuwa followed Jago back through the forest.

'This fight, how bad is it going be?'

'It's going to be great! Two warriors with unsheathed krises ... you won't forget it.'

'Will Gali get hurt? I don't want him getting hurt.'

Jago looked at Yukuwa and quietened down. 'Nah, not against the Mad Macassan. Madya is only good for shoving kids around. Gali will smear him. Don't worry about it. Look!'

He had stopped at a shattered black stump.

'Look at what?'

'The fortress. Our fortress. Mine and Mustari's.'

'This is a fortress?'

'This is a stump, stupid. It got like this in the battle for the fort.'

Yukuwa tried to picture the tree that had grown from the stump. It had to be big, bigger than three Yolngu trees shoved together, but it had been destroyed in one searing blow. Not a Lightning Serpent. Much bigger.

Jago walked through undergrowth to a grassy knoll, steep enough for Yukuwa to need his hands. On the other side the forest fell away, revealing the river sliding slowly before them. They could see the village across the river and the sea behind it. They could look along this side of the river, at the two canoes on the gravel. Theirs, and a sun-bleached older one with a single paddle.

Jago nodded at the other canoe. 'Mustari and me, we would borrow a canoe, paddle it across the river and leave it there.'

'Where is the fortress?' Yukuwa looked about him.

'You're standing on it.'

Yukuwa looked down and realised that many of the rocks around him had corners. He studied the sparse forest he had walked through and saw piles of rocks among the grass. Not natural rocks: chiselled rocks. Broken walls stretched far along the bank.

'We came here a lot. Mustari would charge up the slope, yelling words he said were Balanda. I think he liked playing a Balanda.' Jago's eyes were fixed on Yukuwa's face.

Oh, this is a secret place, like Ragan's brolga glade. Jago is letting you share this place with Mustari. And Mustari is still here.

'Thank you,' Yukuwa said softly.

A smile washed over Jago's lips and grew. 'You like it?'

'I would like Mustari, I think.'

'You would, you would. We would fish, and hunt, and maybe go into the mountains. And battle ...'

'Monkeys!'

Madya was standing at the foot of the knoll with his arms folded. 'What are you doing in my fort?'

'What d'you mean, *your* fort?' Jago shouted.

Madya ran up the knoll and Yukuwa stumbled away. 'This is a Macassan fort. Not for weak little Bugis lovers.'

'I am a Macassan!'

'You play silly little games here.'

'Not silly! We remember the battle.'

'Maybe. Maybe with that dead boy, Mustari. But why do you bring that Monkey here?'

Yukuwa hardened his face.

'What, you get to say who can come here?'

'I have a great grandfather sleeping here.'

Jago faltered.

'Yes. I don't know where. He may be scattered in a thousand places, but he died here. Laba had kin in the Battle of Buton but he licks Balanda boots. I have kin here, at Sombaopu, and I have not lost the anger.'

Jago tried again, quieter. 'Everyone knows about the battle.'

'Hah! You know nothing about Sombaopu, of Hasan-uddin? Nothing!'

'Sombaopu was under a terrible siege ...'

'Sombaopu.' Madya flung his arms out, as if to sweep fifty years aside. 'Here is the last fight. The Balandas have slithered over the spice islands, sunk Sultan Hasanuddin's fleet at Buton, taken the Ujung Pandang fort at Macassar, taken Macassar. There is nothing left to face the Balandas but Sultan Hasanuddin, King of Gowa, with the Holy Cannon of the Macassans – and my great grandfather.'

'Yes, I know ...'

'So they come. The Balandas come up the river and fire their cannon. Aru Palaka of the Kingdom of Bone and his Bugis army is at the wall, there.

'But Hasanuddin is ready. There is the Holy Cannon and many, many soldiers with guns. Here, on this knoll, soldiers can see warships even at sea and they can tell cannons how to aim without the cannon being seen ... What's the matter, Monkey?'

'Nothing, nothing,' said Yukuwa. You were near to battle when you sharpened your spear and stood on the sand to face the Barra tribe. But that was nothing like this. 'And you won?'

Madya's stick drooped in his hand. 'No. Oh, we won this time. Drove Aru Palaka from our walls and the Balanda from our river. But they came back with more ships and men. The palace was hit with thousands of bullets and cannonballs and Sombaopu was ablaze from end to end.

'No more fighting, no more Kingdom of Gowa, and after a little while no more Sultan Hasanuddin. Only Aru Palaka, King of Bone, king of the Bugis for a very long time.'

'And your great grandfather died defending Sombaopu,' said Jago.

'In the flames.'

'Poor soldier.'

'Why?'

'Well … he lost, didn't he?'

'You don't understand, do you? I don't come here to be sorry for him, I come here to wish I was him.'

'But he's dead.'

'That's nothing. I might be dead tomorrow. What do I leave? What am I? I go fishing for fat worms. When I die, I die, nobody remembers me. He still lives. Here two kings fought, and he was part of it. Even now the Balandas remember 1669 and tremble. After Sambaopu they call Macassans a new name – the Fighting Cocks of the East. That is my grandfather's name. Forever.'

Madya stared quietly at the ruins of the fortress.

Jago shifted uncomfortably. 'Well, we better go …'

'Worm Collector, that's me,' Madya said dully.

'But you are his great grandson.'

Madya looked up at Jago. 'Yes, yes. He was a Fighting Cock, then I am one. And so are you. Don't ever forget you are a Macassan.'

'Never.'

'The King of the Bugis defeated the King of the Macassans only because of the Balandas.' Madya broke a twig. 'Tomorrow night there will be no Balandas.'

16 THE DUEL

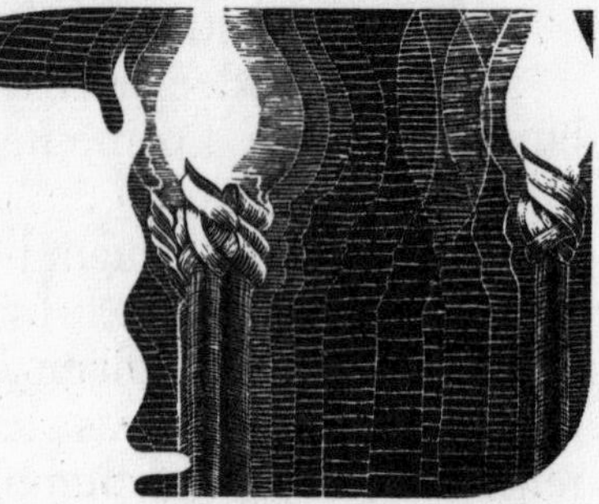

The drummers capered before the Karaeng, slapping the long drums at their waists as they leapt into the air. A folded red cloth on their heads became a cock, continually trying to fly. Yukuwa sat with Dawu by the Karaeng's side, eating rice cakes and expecting someone to realise the mistake and drag him away. Jago's mother was glaring at him from a knot of villagers, but beside her Jago was grinning at him.

The drummers settled in the torchlit sand and were joined by a kecapi player and two men who blew music from a black tube.

Yukuwa looked around for Gali, but he was not on the beach. Nor was Madya.

Young women, wearing full dresses, bright strings and ornamental krises, swayed before the torches. The drummers removed their drums and performed a crouching dance around them, increasing their pace with every attack on the drums, but the women were still gliding gracefully, as if hearing a different music. Farida was not one of the dancers and Yukuwa wondered whether she was with her husband or her brother.

Laba slipped out of the dark, bobbed his head to the Karaeng in apology and flopped beside Yukuwa. He talked softly to Dawu.

'The Great Junk has arrived early. We sail to Macassar tomorrow.'

'Ah, do you need me?' Dawu looked tired.

'No, of course not. I thought you'd like to see the city of Macassar.'

'Is it big? Bigger than the village?'

'Far bigger.'

Dawu smiled wearily and placed his hand on Laba's arm. 'For now, this village is big enough. Take Yukuwa and leave me to make my canoe.'

The evening continued with more dances, songs and stories, but Yukuwa began to notice that people were watching the Karaeng more than the performers. Finally the Karaeng stood and clapped his hands.

'The Kris Contest.'

The drummers caught a very slow rhythm, echoed by the beating of gongs. Two men, strangers to Yukuwa, danced to each other, making each movement deliberate and rigid. They stood on one leg and threatened each other with a raised foot. The drums and gongs increased the beat and the men moved with the rhythm, until they clashed arms once. Then they stopped, stepped aside and the drums and the gongs stilled. Laba stepped into the open space.

Laba beckoned with both hands and Gali came through the crowd with his sheathed kris in his hands. His face was dull.

Madya carried his kris before him, as if he intended to present it to the Karaeng. He flicked the shadow of a smile at someone in the crowd.

Yukuwa saw Jago in the glow of a torch, not grinning any more, just very uncertain. Yukuwa puzzled over the expression, then he understood.

Jago does not know which side he is on, friend or Macassan.

Laba murmured something to the men, then nodded. The krises were drawn from the sheaths and the sheaths were tossed aside. Gali and Madya advanced their krises until the points touched before Laba's face. The curled blades winked in the torchlight.

Laba stepped back.

Neither man moved as they stared into each other's eyes.

'Get on!' someone yelled.

The blades rasp and the men are apart, left hand down, fingers spread on the leg, blades touching, touching, touching ... Madya twists his kris, jabs, Gali steps back, knocks the blade wide. Madya stumbles, recovers, but the smile shadow is gone. Madya clashes, thrusts, driving Gali across the circle.

Gali ducks, catches Madya's blade above his head, breaks for the open ground, stumbles, stumbles again, down on one knee. And the crowd roars! Madya leaps across the sand with the point of his kris ahead and quivering, but Gali's blade is up. Madya slides off and Gali is on his feet ...

A woman sobs once. Farida – Madya's wife, Gali's sister – stares at the men, mouth open, cheeks damp and shining. And across the space is another woman with dead eyes, holding her children so they cannot see. Gali's wife.

The men dance about on the sand, aware of nothing but each other, panting, legs trembling a little ...

Yukuwa remembered a fight he had seen a long while ago on Kingfish Beach. What was the fight about? You can't remember, just that one man had a spear and the other didn't. The man without the spear ran and the man with the spear threw it. The spear missed, and that was the end of the fight.

But *this* ...

Madya's blade sears past Gali's eye. Gali's face flicks from fear to anger. He knocks Madya's arm down, aside, drives him across the space and around the circle. Madya's legs are buckling now. He swings the blade wildly. His eyes are strained white. There's a sound from the crowd, a long, sucking breath.

Madya jabs, finds only Gali's blade. Gali picks at Madya's shirt and there's a touch of blood on the shoulder. The crowd sigh at last.

'Enough!' Laba shouts and steps forward. 'There is blood.'

Gali lowers his kris and begins to bow his head …

And Madya strikes, the blade biting into Gali's side.

The sand swirls next to Yukuwa and Dawu is in the ring, his hand on Madya's wrist. He elbows Madya in the face, hurls him into the crowd.

'That is the end of it!' Laba bellows, and this time it is over.

Dawu saw Farida staring at him. 'He is my friend,' he said.

Yukuwa was nodding slowly, feeling an emptiness.

Jago stayed at the edge of the crowd, watching some of the men slapping Madya on the back, laughing among themselves. He hesitated, then came across to Yukuwa.

Gali was being eased down to the sand, with his wife and his sister supporting him. He kept looking at the kris that stuck out of his side. Laba held the hilt and was trying to ease it from his body.

'I didn't know it would be like this,' Jago's words trickled away.

Part Three

17 MACASSAR

The *Gaddong* slid past the river in the gleam of early morning. Yukuwa watched the ruined fortress back into a shadowed tangle of old forest, then the old forest giving way to young forest, trees almost as tall as old forest but slender and more tightly packed.

'That's the edge of old Macassar.' Laba stood behind Yukuwa. 'Before the Balandas.'

Madya looked up from the rope he was working, but he said nothing.

Nobody was saying much today. The crew had hauled up the sails, pulled in the anchors and sailed slowly and silently away from the village, as if they were asleep. Gali was not on the boat, but he was there. Like One-Eye at the Beach of Trees.

No, Yukuwa thought. Not like One-Eye. Gali was still alive.

'Used to be a hundred thousand people in Macassar,' Laba said. A village chopped into the young forest.

Tale smiled softly, as if he was staring at something nobody else could see. 'Macassans, Bugis, Malays, Chinese, trading in spices, scented wood, rice, fine china ... Macassar was the centre of the world.'

The village went on, and on.

Yukuwa frowned. 'What is a hundred thousand? More than thirty?'

Remember when the Barra tribe and the tribe from the flint quarry both visited at the Beach of Trees? Never seen such a crowd! The beach was lined with shelters, shouts of children drove the birds away and smoke was always getting in your eyes. That was thirty.

'Of course it's more than thirty!' Jago laughed. 'You don't know anything.'

All right, it was more. That was before the Macassans. Thirty was the crew of the *Gaddong*. What was the village? Five *Gaddong*s?

'Such a smart boy,' said Tale. 'Well, Jago, you tell us. What's a hundred thousand?'

'A shoal of fish.' Jago sniffed.

'You have never seen it either. It is the stars on a good night.'

Yukuwa nodded. 'The termites in a termite hill.'

The houses were becoming bigger, then their wooden walls became white stone. The *Gaddong* slipped between a reef and a small green island and nosed towards a grey cliff with a flag rippling in the breeze.

'That's Ujung Pandang – Cape Lookout,' said Jago.

'Not any more,' said Tale. 'Now it's Fort Rotterdam. It's not ours, it belongs to the Balandas.'

A fortress, Yukuwa thought. Like Sombaopu, but more. Made – *made* of stone. Yukuwa squinted at the grey stone cliff and saw the seams of the builders. Roofs of great houses towered behind the walls.

'We should take it back!' said Madya loudly.

'Go ahead,' said Tale with a shrug.

'That's your trouble, you don't do anything.'

'Shut up, Madya.' Laba was rubbing his thumb nervously.

'Worried about the cannon?' Tale said.

Yukuwa looked at the regular slots in the top of the cliff. See the black circles. Cannon. Pointed at you, boy! Dawu should be with you. No, you should be with Dawu.

'Hope they rot in there,' Jago said.

'That's enough,' Laba said.

'You think they can hear?' Madya said.

'I don't want to find out.'

The *Gaddong* slid past black-sailed fishing boats towards a stone and wood waterfront. There was a forest of tall poles in the water far ahead.

'It's there,' Tale said.

'Get the *Gaddong* as close as you can,' Laba said. 'We're early.'

The *Gaddong* slid slowly across the glassy water of Macassar Harbour. The mainsail was taken down, slowing the boat to a ripple.

'So big ...' Yukuwa hung onto a rope.

The *Gaddong* was a tadpole, a canoe. She was moving among great wooden ships at anchor, so motionless they might have been carved cliffs. Their bows and their sterns reared above the *Gaddong*, almost as high as the tripod mast. The bowsprits thrust so far over the water an old crocodile could rest in the shadow.

'Balandas?'

'Macassan cargo ships, that's all.'

The *Gaddong* approached the greatest ship of them all. The China Junk sat among the Macassan cargo ships like a black swan among a drift of ducklings. The black stern, taller than the stone buildings on the waterfront, leered down at Yukuwa as the *Gaddong* slid past.

The *Gaddong* turned to move along the side of the China Junk, and the remaining sail was taken down. Yukuwa felt as though he was walking next to a high wooden wall, and on the wall two strange men were studying him. Beyond them three massive masts poked at the clouds.

Laba said: 'Now,' and Madya dropped an anchor.

One of the strange men pointed at Yukuwa and said something, and the other man laughed.

Yukuwa shook his head. Oh fine. These funny-sounding men have their hair plaited into a black rope running from the back of the head. And their skin? It's not black, not even brown. It's the colour of dried grass. And *they* are laughing at you!

Laba said something to the strange men and one of them replied, pointing at the waterfront. Yukuwa did not understand a word.

'We're first.' Laba looked at a fat canoe being paddled towards them from the shore. He dismissed it and hurried to the *Gaddong*'s single canoe. 'We must make use of this. Come on, come on.'

Macassar struck at Yukuwa while he and Jago were still paddling Laba and Tale towards the shore. A curl of air wafted across the canoe and he picked up the stench of urine, manure, rotten fish and something that made his eyes water. Worse than the week-dead wallaby he'd found in the bush back of Kingfish Bay, worse than the beached dugong.

'Bloody buffalo. Why don't they clean things up?' said Laba.

Two large black birds were tearing at the carcass a spear-throw away. The tide gave it a ghastly touch of life, moving one leg as water slopped over it.

The canoe touched pebbles and Jago leaped out to haul it out of the water. Laba strode into the cluttered streets, leaving the others to follow him as best they could.

The smell remained bad, but never as bad as it had been. Buffalo and fish were replaced by rotting wood, vegetables and the mingling sweat of a small shouting crowd, meat burning on a fire, tobacco smoke.

Yukuwa wrinkled his nose. The smell is all right, I guess. At least it's different. But the rest of it is like walking between rocky cliffs, never a tree, a bush, or even a clump of weeds. Your feet feel timber, ash, grit, hot stones, but never soft sand and damp soil.

He passed houses of old bamboo with palm-leaf roofs – not much different to the shelters of the Beach of Trees. But others were made of many-coloured wood or stone, with holes of glinting material that looked like water in a pool. With every step the rushing crowd increased. He was in the termite hill.

But at least Jago was with him, explaining things. He now knew what shops and glass were.

Laba shouldered his way into a musky house and a dried grass man rose from his table in annoyance. 'He's not here.'

'Where is he?'

'In the temple. He doesn't want to be disturbed.'

Laba waved his group back into the street.

The temple was a street away, a red and gold building in the clutter of grey shops. A huge demon glared through a row of smoke sticks at Yukuwa.

Yukuwa thought, Balanda! and shuffled backwards.

'It's not real,' Jago said in boredom.

'I know that,' Yukuwa lied. All right, it's no more than a painted carving, like a bark painting or One-Eye's grave-post.

He curled his lip at the demon and walked quickly past.

Tale started to walk into the temple with the plate of trepang but Laba stopped him. 'We wait.'

Yukuwa watched several men walking into the temple, all with their hair plaited from the back of their heads.

'That's so they can be pulled into heaven when they die,' Jago said.

'Ah.'

All with skin the colour of dried grass, Yukuwa thought. It's like Dawu says. The Macassans live near sunset so they are brown. We live under the high sun so we are black. The Chinese must live even closer to the sunset, as they are not getting much sun.

After a while two dried grass men walked from the temple, talking.

Laba stepped forward and smiled at the tall lean man in the blue coat. 'I hope you have had a fine voyage, Li Khoo.'

Li Khoo smiled but turned the smile into a grimace. 'The wind is fine, Laba, the food is bad – nothing changes. The Canton merchants think we can sail their ships on two grains of rice.'

'Oh, ah,' the plump man in the shiny red coat rushed in. 'More important, Laba. Have *you* had a good voyage?'

Laba motioned Tale forward and Tale removed the cloth covering the plate with a flourish. The five red trepang were pressed towards the agent. The agent looked at them, raised his eyes to Laba and prodded one trepang judiciously with a finger. He drew a small knife from the folds of his white trousers and carefully cut himself a slice.

Li Khoo was more interested in Yukuwa than the trepang. 'African?'

'Marege,' Laba said.

'I have seen boys like that in Madagascar. Not from Madagascar?'

'No,' said Yukuwa. 'Marege.'

The agent nodded. 'Marege. I knew the taste. Not the best, but they'll do.' He offered a slice to Li Khoo. 'How many?'

'Maybe two hundred piculs.'

The agent smiled. 'Twelve tons? I had better see what you've got, then.' He put his hand on Laba's elbow and began to walk him towards the waterfront. 'The price for trepang is down these days, but I'll see what we can do ...'

Jago nudged Yukuwa aside. 'We don't want to go back yet, do we? There's things to see in Macassar.'

'Well ...' Yukuwa watched Laba and Tale walk round a corner with the dried grass people.

'I can show you the Balandas ...'

Yukuwa looked at Jago. You do not want to see the Balandas. They have been a cold wind on your neck from the waters of Old People's Camp to here. Balandas keep demons in their cannons to sink ships, kill men, destroy fortresses. No, you do not want to see them.

'Well, I think ...'

You have been scared of the *Gaddong*. Scared of the open sea, and the village, and of Macassar. You have even been scared of the carved demon in the Chinese temple. But now? No, not any more. Because you have seen them, lived with them, walked round in them.

You *have* to see the Balandas, or you will always be afraid of them.

'All right.'

18 THE BALANDA

Jago darted through the steaming lanes of the Macassar waterfront, laughing, whooping, with Yukuwa at his heels. Until he burst into a street and ran into a man.

A strange man. Stranger than the dried grass men from China. This man wore black from his wide hat to his shoes, with a piece of stained white material around his neck. His face was a pale grey with eyes glinting like water-washed pebbles as he moved his head.

He plucked Jago from his stomach and said a few odd words.

Jago tried to twist free.

'What have we here?' the man said in Macassan, but with an awkward accent. Then he took off his eyes.

Yukuwa could not breathe.

The man in black put his eyes back, looked at Yukuwa and smiled. He let Jago go. 'Africa?'

Not eyes, glass. Windows for eyes. 'Marege.'

Jago ran a few steps and stopped.

'The trepang coast. You are a long way from home.'

'Yes.' Yukuwa bobbed his head. A long, long way.

'So am I.' The man shrugged a little. Suddenly he and Yukuwa were smiling at each other; strangers, but in a stranger place.

'C'mon, Yukuwa.'

'I have never been there.' The man in black sat on the edge of a step. 'I have read that it is a harsh desert, where nothing grows.'

'Desert?' Yukuwa shook his head. 'No, no, we have rivers, flood plains, forests – forests alive with food, yams, apples, wallabies – sometimes you can eat yourself fat by walking around the campfire. There's fish – there's always fish – and the sky is full of birds.'

The man in black sucked his lip. 'My people have sailed along the west coast of your land, gone ashore. They all said the land was barren and useless.'

Silly grey men, they cannot see through the windows. 'Not our land.'

'Yukuwa! Come on!'

'Not New Holland? But of course you call it something else. What?'

'Marege.'

'No.' The man in black pointed at Jago, who was making strange signs. 'That is what the Macassans call it. What do you people call it?'

Yukuwa shrugged. 'Land of the Yolngu ...'

Jago finally shouted. 'Yukuwa, he is Balanda!'

Yukuwa shied from the man, but the man just kept on smiling.

'Yes, of course. Hollander ...'

Jago pulled Yukuwa off-balance and into the street. The man in black lifted his eyes from Yukuwa, then sprang to his feet, clutching Yukuwa and Jago by their shoulders, and dragged them aside.

'Let go!' Jago fumbled for his kris. 'You ...'

His voice was drowned by a clattering on the cobbles, a creaking and heavy panting. Two horses, their bodies gleaming with sweat, careered past the huddle on the step. The horses were pulling something.

Yukuwa stepped backwards. Like the village's goat cart.

Hah! If this is like a goat cart, then the *Gaddong* is like a bark canoe. A coloured open boat on wheels, taller than a buffalo. And there is a man with a face full of hair, sitting high on the bow, cracking a long strip of leather over the horses – driving them away. But these horses are tied to the boat and no matter how hard they run the boat and the men stay behind ...

Suddenly the strange race finished. Just like that. A fat man in the middle of the boat saw the man in black and shouted at the hairy man. The hairy man pulled at other leather strips and the horses stopped running. The fat man was grander than the Karaeng, with a three-cornered hat, more white hair than Gathul could grow in ten seasons, and a large blue and gold coat. And the woman sitting beside him was awesome. Her face was as white as the belly of a turtle, but her cheeks glowed crimson. She was sinking to her neck in a sea of red and white material that sparkled in the sun. There was no sign of her legs.

'Hals!' The fat man shouted at the man in black.

Hals touched the rim of his hat.

The fat man shouted briefly at Hals, then prodded the hairy man with a gold-tipped stick. The hairy man cracked his leather strip and the horses clattered down the street.

Hals looked unhappily after the fat man, then spread his hands. 'I must leave now.' He stepped away from Yukuwa.

'Goodbye Hals,' said Yukuwa.

Hals stopped and turned. 'Pieter Hals. What is your name?'

'Yukuwa.'

'Yukuwa. I will remember.'

'Where are you going, Pieter Hals?'

'To do a job. A bad job. You look after yourselves.' Hals was trying to smile.

'We look after ourselves pretty good,' said Jago. 'I can take Yukuwa everywhere. I know Macassar.'

'Fine, just ...'

'I am Macassan.'

The tired smile disappeared. 'You stay away from Fort Rotterdam, you hear?'

Jago blinked.

'You hear?'

'Yes, yes.'

'All right.' Hals walked stiffly away.

'That was a Balanda?' Yukuwa watched him go.

'Yes, and you were talking to him!'

'So were you.'

'Just to show him I wasn't afraid.'

'What was there to be afraid of?'

'You just don't know ... What about the fat shouter? Everyone in that carriage was Balanda.'

Yukuwa thought of the grey face of Hals. How far west would his home be? Maybe beyond sunset.

'Not bad enough for you?' Jago said. 'You want to see the real mean ones?'

Yukuwa followed with a shrug. Jago's terrors weren't real. Balandas had no demons, just funny clothes and land-boats. The sea was worse.

But he slowed when Jago led him up to a dark rippled stone wall, with cannon tasting the breeze high over his head.

'Where are we going?'

'Fort Rotterdam.'

19 FORT ROTTERDAM

Yukuwa stopped. 'That Balanda – Hals – he said not to go there.'

Jago hissed. 'We don't do what the Balandas say.'

'Hals was warning us. Maybe ...'

'Mustari and me, we have been all over Rotterdam.'

Yukuwa stopped. How can you argue with a spirit boy?

'Dozens of times.' Jago marched defiantly to a corner, then turned to Yukuwa with his hands on his hips. 'Well?'

Yukuwa slowly breathed out, but he went.

They walked between the wall and the sea for a few steps, then turned towards the main entrance. It was crowded with Balandas. Men with trimmed beards, broad hats, high hats, squashed hats, dark coats, baggy trousers, boots, shoes. They talked with women in tight hair covers and dresses that could hide a mob of wallabies. At the side of the entrance a few men with long knives – far longer than krises – and metal sticks, looked grimly at the crowd.

'See them?' Jago said happily. 'Mean Balandas, soldiers with swords and muskets. Cut your heart out quick as look at you.'

Yukuwa moved from the wall to stare at a Balanda with a stained white moustache until he was waved away. He backed into a jostling crowd of Chinese and Bugis, and was pushed inside the fort.

Inside the walls, great stone buildings shouldered each other, hurling black shadows across the dusty ground. Many of the windows had bars instead of glass. Balandas walked about the enclosure, the men prodding the ground with polished sticks and the women holding their men by an arm. The other people shuffled out of the way. Everyone seemed to be moving towards a distant corner.

'Hoy!' A fat Balanda with a red face stood behind him, shouting.

'Um?' Yukuwa lifted his hands helplessly.

The Balanda clicked his tongue and hit Yukuwa's legs with his stick. Yukuwa yelped and skipped quickly away. He stopped after a few steps and touched the burning pain in his legs, more puzzled than angry.

He felt eyes on him and slowly lifted his head.

Ten men pressed against a wall of iron bars, staring at him with an intense desperation. They were Macassans, like the men from the *Gaddong*, but their clothes were dirty. They were dirty and tired. And frightened.

Yukuwa stiffened. No, they aren't looking at you, they are staring *through* you. At that distant corner. And it's not only them. There's a wall of stone next to them and then more bars and more staring men, and then more bars and men ...

Oh.

They can't leave. None of them. There are walls behind them, a roof over them. They are fish in a trap.

Suddenly Yukuwa was very afraid. More afraid of what he saw than of the endless sea, of One-eye, of the shark. He felt the old lizard twisting in his belly.

'Come on!' Jago dived from a crowd, snatched at Yukuwa and towed him past two soldiers and halfway up some steps set into the wall of the fort. 'I have to keep looking after you, like a sister. More trouble than you're worth.'

'I wasn't doing anything.'

'You didn't have to. See the guards we passed?'

'Um, those?'

'Yeah, those. They were talking about you.'

'Why?'

'They think you're an escaped slave.'

'What's a slave?'

'Don't you know anything at all? A slave is someone who is captured and made to work for someone else for nothing for the rest of his life.'

'I wouldn't.'

'You wouldn't? What would you do?'

'I'd leave. I'd run away.'

'And you'd be a runaway slave. They'd throw you into a cell down there with all the other prisoners. Maybe keep you in chains.'

'No!' Yukuwa shook his head and stumbled backwards.

Jago caught him, surprise on his face. 'All right. You're not there, you'll never be there.'

Yukuwa looked down at the cells and the silent men behind the bars and shivered. 'Why?' He was whispering. 'Why are they there?'

'They are prisoners of the Balandas.'

'Like slaves?'

'Worse. That is punishment. They have done something the Balandas don't like, so the Balandas punish them by throwing them into the cells.'

'For how long?'

'I don't know, years and years.'

Yukuwa watched the prisoners staring at the raised wooden square in the distant corner.

Remember Bawi? He had thrown a spear at a kangaroo

in the long grass and killed the Widow's husband. One of the husband's brothers had speared Bawi in the leg. You had thought it a terrible punishment, but Bawi had been hunting wallabies within a moon. But this? You cannot walk, see new things in a new day, feel the grass between your toes. This is death.

Drums beat around the fort and people moved towards the wooden square. But these drums sounded completely different to the wild drums of the village. In the village the drums laughed. Here they marched slowly.

'Oh.' Jago stood up.

'Hey.' A soldier standing on the parapet saw Jago's head. 'What d'you think you're doing?'

Yukuwa stood with Jago and prepared to run. The soldier's boots were crunching towards his eyes, and another soldier was standing beside a cannon with a small fire on a stick. The cannon was far bigger than the one on the *Gaddong*, with a pile of large black balls beside it.

The Balanda with the fire called to the other Balanda, and dismissed Jago and Yukuwa with a wave of his hand.

The first Balanda stopped a step from Yukuwa's head. 'All right, you can watch. Learn a lesson. But don't come any closer.'

The rhythm of the drums changed, drawing Yukuwa's eyes to the square.

A man in black climbed onto the square with a book in his hands.

Hals.

A struggling man was being pushed onto the square. He did not seem to be able to use his hands. Hals stepped up to the struggling man and said something. The man shouted at Hals and jerked his head forward. Hals stepped back and read from his book while a soldier put a loop of rope around the man's neck.

'What are they doing?'

The man stopped struggling and shouted at the crowd and the crowd shouted back. The soldier pushed the man from the high square.

'What ...' And then he knew. He stared at the man and the roar of the crowd became the roar of blood in his ears. He could feel the flesh of his face quiver.

The man began to dance in the air.

Yukuwa jerked his eyes away.

And saw the firestick touch the back of the cannon. The cannon roared, spat heavy smoke and the two soldiers stood with hands over their ears, mouths open and eyes wide.

When Yukuwa looked back the man was motionless on the end of the rope.

He wanted to run until the wind had scoured his eyes. But he stood on the stone step and stared.

20 AMBUSH

Yukuwa was still numb as Jago led him back to the waterfront and the cheerful crowd seemed to be roaring with laughter at him. There was another ship anchored beyond the Great Junk: three masts, bigger than the Macassan cargo ships but not quite as big as the Junk.

'Balanda,' said Jago dully.

'Where?' Yukuwa avoided Jago's eyes.

'There. The ship out there.'

'Oh.' They were everywhere. There was no escape.

Laba waved at them from the *Gaddong* and sent Tale to fetch them.

Tale's smile died when he saw their faces. 'Trouble? Eat something bad? Don't want to talk?'

They stepped into the canoe and paddled in silence.

The *Gaddong* was rubbing fenders with the Junk, with the crew passing the trepang up from the hold to the Chinese.

Laba was talking to Junk captain Li Khoo and the agent but he broke away to help Jago aboard. Yukuwa saw that he now wore a Balanda weapon, a pistol, next to his kris. He looked grave.

'You know ... ?' Jago started.

But Laba turned back to Li Khoo. 'Almost done.'

Li Khoo nodded as he studied the Balanda ship.

He is afraid of them, thought Yukuwa bleakly. Yukuwa saw the square holes in the side, and the glint of the cannon behind them. A huge red, white and blue flag trailed from the stern and other flags flew from the top of the three masts, even from the bowsprit. A fat boat had been lowered from the deck and men in blue were running about, giving orders. The Balandas looked as if they were about to attack.

But Li Khoo was shaking his head. 'They have lost many men on the voyage.' He passed his hand before his nose.

Yukuwa sniffed and the Balanda ship looked different. The flags were still there, a golden woman leaned from the bow, but the ten sails were stowed loosely and one edge of the mainsail dangled like a large dead bird. The deck was cluttered and stained. The hull was marked by rust, rot and rough seas. More than that, the ship stank of rotten food, bilge and human waste.

Suddenly the Balandas were vulnerable.

'The Balandas will lose more in Macassar.' The agent nodded at the thin, ill grey men being loaded into the boat.

'Good. Less Balandas,' said Li Khoo in deep satisfaction.

The agent looked surprised. 'Balandas, Hollanders? But they're not. The Hollanders will take anyone to run their ships. Germans, Danish, maybe even a Portuguese, English ...'

'English? They come to China with opium now, for our tea. No difference, they're all Balandas.'

The agent and Li Khoo left the *Gaddong* with the last basket of trepang, nodding at a still grave-faced Laba.

Laba held his expression until the agent finally left the *Gaddong* for the China Junk, then he beamed. 'A good deal, a great deal!' He went into his cabin in the *Gaddong* with a soiled white bag, but he didn't see the agent slap Li Khoo on the back.

The crew moved the *Gaddong* away from the junk and anchored again. A boy paddled a boat up to the *Gaddong* and waited, grinning.

Laba called for Tale and Tale ducked before the hut, rising with a small bag that clinked.

'That much?' said Jago.

'I don't gamble, I don't drink, I don't go upstairs in the bars, so I don't owe Laba. Laba owes me.'

Other crewmen crouched before the hut and rose with smaller bags.

Tale watched the payments with sympathy. 'Some of the crew won't get *any* money from this voyage,' he said to Yukuwa. 'They owe it all to Laba before the *Gaddong* leaves the village. But Laba will lend them money today so they will sail with him next time.'

Yukuwa watched the Balanda boat move past the *Gaddong*, the paddlers not looking where they were going, facing the ship they had left and hauling long paddles. They looked eager, grinning through their beards, but men at the bow and the stern sagged against each other, no teeth, no blood in their skin, hollows around the eyes.

There were no demons in these Balandas.

'Madya? Where's Madya?' Laba poked his head out of his little cabin.

'Saw him walking into a bar, before,' Tale shrugged.

'He hasn't the money for it.'

'He wasn't alone. He was with some men talking about a rebel the Balandas were going to hang.'

'That was this afternoon,' Jago said bleakly.

'You see this?' Laba said sharply.

'We got caught in the crowd.'

'That's dangerous.'

'They were talking about rescuing him,' said Tale.

'Well, they just didn't, did they?'

'It's none of our business.' Laba gave some coins to Jago. 'Go ashore, have fun and forget about it.'

'Just stay away from the waterfront.' Tale was watching the Balanda boat crunch ashore.

Jago nodded and shambled towards the fat canoe.

Yukuwa moved after him but Laba caught him by the shoulder. 'You are part of the crew.' He pressed a couple of coins into Yukuwa's hands.

'Take it, spend up big.' The smile faded. 'Just look after Jago.'

The crewmen followed the Balanda seamen into crowded houses that smelt of mouldy wheat and sweat. Several women waved at them from top windows.

Jago walked away from the waterfront with Yukuwa by his side, but with no direction. He stopped outside a white-walled house with its windows filled with bright objects. Jago looked at them for a while, shrugged and strode inside. Inside were walls of jars, tins, barrels and an enormous pink woman, fanning herself with a large feather.

'Hello boys,' she said in that odd accent. 'What can I do for you?'

Jago looked at his coin and slowly nodded. He passed it to the woman without a trace of a smile and pointed at the bright green, yellow, red, brown objects.

The woman put all the things in a bag and Jago walked outside.

'What's that?' Yukuwa asked.

'What?'

'That.'

Jago looked at the bag in his hands as if he had not known he carried it. 'Sweets,' he said, offering Yukuwa a yellow stick.

Yukuwa followed Jago through the Balanda shops, through the Chinese shops, touching the yellow stick and tasting his finger. He put the yellow stick in his mouth and sucked. Almost as sweet as wild honey, but with something else, some sort of fruit.

They drifted out of the shops and along a wide street, with tall palms forming a shifting green tunnel. Beyond the palms were big houses of white stone, each one set apart and surrounded by cropped grass, flowers, palms and stone walls. The Balanda street was almost as peaceful as the bush in the afternoon, but it finished against the dark walls of Fort Rotterdam.

They turned away together without a word. Jago led Yukuwa past the stone houses, the wooden houses, the bamboo shacks, to where the town petered out. There were a few houses on stilts but they were leaning, waiting for the fresh wind to push them into the mud of the paddy and the jungle.

'There's nothing here,' Yukuwa said.

'Yes.'

Yukuwa nodded. Sometimes he walked into the bush to work things out.

Jago sat on a log. 'Why did he say that?'

Yukuwa sat beside him. 'Who?'

'A Macassan gets hanged. But Laba says it's none of our business.'

'There's nothing we can do.'

'There's got to be.'

A black shadow shambled along the path, stopping, rocking slightly a few paces from the log.

'Hello, Hals,' said Yukuwa.

'Yukuwa!' Hals reached the log in a short rush and sat heavily. 'What have you got there?'

Yukuwa smelled something bitter on Hals' breath as he offered Jago's bag to him.

Jago snatched the bag from Hals' hands. 'You killed him.'

Hals lowered his head. 'You were there.'

Jago was silent.

'I didn't kill him. I was trying to help.'

A man started to sing across Macassar as the sun touched the roofs.

'The mosque,' said Jago. He began to twist his body, to find Mecca but stopped. 'Yeah, I saw that.'

'He didn't want my kind of help.'

Closer, a bell rang heavily, fighting the singer for the sunset.

'My church. I should be there, but I cannot face them.'

'You're a holy man?' Yukuwa was astonished.

'A predikant, a minister. No, not so holy. The company brings me here, pays me, tells me what to do and I do it. Not so holy.'

'He spat on you,' said Jago.

'Yes.'

Jago was silent.

Pieter Hals sat on the log for a while, then he slowly pulled himself to his feet, staggered a little and wandered away.

Yukuwa and Jago stayed on the log until the sky darkened, talking only a little.

Jago looked at his final sweet and suddenly hurled it out into the paddy. 'We'd better get back.'

Yukuwa followed Jago through some derelict buildings and faltered. Something was wrong.

Jago stepped ahead – and a skinny man with a drawn kris erupted from the earth before him. He clutched Jago by the hair and pressed the blade against his throat. 'Who are you?'

Yukuwa stumbled backwards, his eyes wide.

'Anyone know these?'

Another three men kicked free from the undergrowth and one of them grinned at Yukuwa. 'Allo, Monkey.'

'All right, Madya, are they trouble?'

'Nah, they're from my old boat.'

The kris was taken from Jago's throat.

'This is a dangerous place,' said the skinny man. 'Why are you here?'

'I been here before,' Jago said, a little shakily.

'No Balanda law here,' said Madya.

'That's why we're here. Gali took me here once. He'd point over the paddies and say that was where the city of Macassar used to stretch.'

'Gali said that?' said Madya. 'Gali?'

'He said that was when the Macassans ruled the sea.'

Madya shook his head.

'Yes,' the skinny man said. 'Before the Balandas came and said that the Macassans must leave Macassar. With the Java men and the Malays.'

'Balandas killed Macassar.' Madya looked up. 'Now they kill Macassans.'

'The hanging,' Jago said.

'Yes.' The skinny man frowned. 'Did you see it?'

'Yes.'

'We couldn't stop it. But we can make the Balandas pay.'

'Right now!' Madya pointed his kris at a tall man picking his way towards the gleam of the paddy.

'Yes!' The skinny man charged through the undergrowth with Madya and the other men lurching after him.

Yukuwa saw the hat, saw the wandering walk, and shouted, 'No! Leave him alone!'

Hals jerked his head up, his glasses glinting. He stumbled, started to run to the houses and was caught. He staggered as the men swirled around him, and then fell from them. Someone shouted from the Balanda houses and the men broke away.

Yukuwa ran to Hals, crying in Yolngu: 'Sorry, sorry, sorry.' He stopped by his hat, a step away from the hump of his body. Hals rolled a little and looked up at Yukuwa.

Perhaps Hals was all right, perhaps he could still help. Like at Kingfisher Beach, so long ago. He dropped to his knees.

Three, four, five ... No, too many, too much. He bent over Hals, helpless, and Hals smiled sadly up at him.

More shouts from the houses and two sudden reports.

Hals' eyes flicked wide. 'No, no. You go away. Away!' He flopped a limp hand at Yukuwa.

'Come on!' Jago was pulling at his arm, staring at the houses.

Yukuwa allowed himself to be dragged from the man, still looking back at his face. Then he saw flashes and heard more hollow explosions. The Balandas were firing muskets at him! He ran past Jago and dived into the undergrowth.

Jago deliberately tripped him and fell across him. The panic passed when he understood what Jago was doing and lay still.

A group of men ran from the houses, some to gather round Hals, the others to spread along the paddies and jungle. A man shouted and pointed at a single shadow splashing across a distant paddy. It seemed that every Balanda fired at the shadow, the flashes rippling in the dark. The shadow spun and fell into the water. Two men walked easily to where the man had fallen as the other men looked sadly at Hals.

Hals was lifted carefully, even tenderly, onto the shoulders of six men and carried slowly towards Balanda Macassar. Behind them the two soldiers shoved at a man with their rifle butts. Madya clutched at his bloody shoulder as he stumbled along. There was pain in his eyes, but this was almost washed away by the fear.

'They will be looking for us, now,' Jago said. 'We can't go back.'

Yukuwa nodded without hearing. He was seeing what lay ahead for Madya: the crowded cells, watching other men stepping onto the high floor for the waiting rope. Until it was his turn.

21 THE GHOST PEOPLE

Jago dragged Yukuwa to his feet as the sound of the Balandas faded away. They ran into the dark, away from the low lights and echoes of the city, stopping only when all they could hear was a single clicking insect.

'Can you hear? Is anyone following?' He peered into the dark.

'Nobody.' Yukuwa breathed heavily. 'What do we do now?'

Jago squeezed his eyes shut. 'Don't know. Bad, very bad. Wish – wish Mustari was here.'

Yukuwa looked at him sharply. 'He's not.' And neither is Dawu.

'No, he's not.'

'Can we walk back to the village?'

Jago shook his head. 'Balandas could be everywhere now.'

'No way of getting to the *Gaddong*?'

'You're mad.'

'We got to do something.'

'Okay, *you* do something. You're the big hunter.'

Yukuwa flinched, but he saw a dark shadow through the trees and remembered the mountains he'd seen from the *Gaddong*, mountains that disappeared into the cloud. 'There,' he said, and began to walk.

All right, maybe it's no good, but it is better than thinking about Hals or – worse – Madya. And it's far better than waiting for help from a spirit boy.

Yukuwa saw the dull firelight of a small village and moved towards it, but Jago pulled back.

'Why? The Balandas can't be there.'

'Spies. They can be anywhere.'

Yukuwa looked at him.

'What?' Jago was rubbing his throat. The hanging shadowed them both.

'Stay in the forest, then?'

'Better. Until we know what's happening.'

They camped by a stream near the mountains. Yukuwa lay under a tall tree, listening to the soft shivering of the fat leaves, the cry of a night bird, the rustle of a hurrying animal. Foreign sounds, but when he closed his eyes and breathed the damp forest air he was almost at home.

'Why so happy?' Jago muttered.

'It's peaceful here.'

'In the forest? It's dangerous. There are bands of monkey robbers and the poison darts of the Toala – ghost people. You sleep, I'll watch.'

But when Yukuwa woke, Jago was sprawled against a tree snoring quietly.

Jago stretched as the sun filtered through the leaves and opened an eye. 'I'm hungry,' he said. The hanging and the murder were moons away.

'So am I.'

'So, what are you going to do about it?'

'Me? It's your island.'

'You're the hunter. I can remember how you got that crocodile.'

Yukuwa looked at Jago, then sighed and started to look for a straight branch for a spear haft.

@

They followed cart tracks through the forest, hiding at any approaching sound. Jago took a few green bananas and some uncooked rice from the land around a village, and then they were alone in the forest.

Not quite alone. A rage of chattering animals swept through the tree tops one night, like hairy little people.

'Monkeys,' said Jago and drew his kris.

Yukuwa threw his spear and missed. A monkey threw a nut at Yukuwa and hit him on the head.

Jago didn't laugh, just shrugged. 'I cannot eat it, anyway.'

Next day Yukuwa surprised himself by spearing a dozy bird, but it took him four hours to get a fire going to cook it. He taught Jago how to carry a fire stick after that.

They were wondering how bugs and centipedes would taste when they found a waterfall battering its way down a broad rock slope. They found dark mottled fish in the deep pool at its foot; Yukuwa speared one, Jago chased another onto a rock ledge.

They wrapped them in leaves and cooked them, sniffing them cooking in the fire and grinning at each other.

In the late afternoon they swam in the pool, surrounded by tall glistening trees and huge luminous butterflies. Balandas did not exist for them now.

But there were others in these forests. 'What are these ghost people?' asked Yukuwa.

'You only hear about them,' Jago said with a shrug. 'They are Toala, the forest people. Hunt with poison darts, but nobody sees them. Some villages put rice, krises, sarongs, pots outside their doors at sunset and next morning there are pelts, meat and beadwork instead. So they are ghost people.'

Yukuwa shivered in the cold water.

'Ah, they're nothing,' said Jago, floating on his back. 'Like I say, nobody sees them. This is good, hey?'

Yukuwa patted his solid stomach. 'Oh, yes.' Wonder what Dawu's doing. Worrying? Wonder what Ragan's doing.

'Wish Mustari was here,' said Jago.

A smile crept over Yukuwa's face. No, we don't want anyone.

'We never did anything like this,' Jago said. 'It's better than the village. Hey?'

'Better.' This is ours. Not Mustari's, thought Yukuwa.

'Better than Macassar?'

'Much better.' Not Dawu's.

'Better than Old People's Camp!' Looking quickly across at Yukuwa.

'Yes.' Not Ragan's.

'You're a pretty good hunter, aren't you?'

'Well ...' It's ours. Jago the warrior, Yukuwa the hunter.

'You got that bird, you got that fish.'

'Yes.' Here, in this pool, in this forest, you are a great hunter.

'You got that crocodile!'

So long as you don't leave the pool. Yukuwa sank his head in the water. 'I'm not really that ...'

'And Dawu's a great fisherman. He's becoming a part of the village.'

Yukuwa watched an iridescent blue butterfly, broad as two open hands, wafting over his head.

'It's just that ...' Jago kicked an arc of water into the air. 'Ah, the village gets to be so boring. Why don't you stay?'

'Stay here for ever?' Yukuwa poked the water and grinned.

'Stay on my island, Celebes. Become a Macassan. We could do this all the time. Look around, there's nothing like this in Marege is there?'

Yukuwa watched the water catching the sun high on

the rock slope, cascading towards him, crashing off a gleaming stone shoulder, filling the air with tiny jewels.

'No, not like this.'

'C'mon, stay.'

Yukuwa smiled, and thought of the dancing on the beaches, the fishing in the floating house, and ...

'And the Balandas will never catch us.'

The man dancing in the air ...

'Let's catch a fish,' said Yukuwa.

'It's just ...' Jago groped for words, shrugged and swam after Yukuwa.

They stayed for a few days by the waterfall before moving towards the mountains. They were walking between the rock hills that thrust from the forest when Yukuwa saw a faint animal track in the clay.

'What is it?' Yukuwa squatted and moved a few blades of grass from the track.

Jago shrugged. 'Don't know. Big enough to eat? Hoh!' He suddenly stumbled back.

Yukuwa looked up at a flat-nosed man, wearing only a bark loin cloth and carrying a length of bamboo, a quiver of long darts. He had made no sound at all in approaching them.

'Hello.' Yukuwa slowly rose.

'Toala,' Jago warned.

The Toala was darker than Jago but no taller. He was deeply interested in the spear Yukuwa had made from a rock shard, a vine and a shaved branch.

'Hello,' Yukuwa tried again.

'They don't speak Macassan. You can't speak to him.'

The Toala pointed at his darts and at Yukuwa's spear as if to say 'We are both hunters.' The paw print, said the Toala's hands, is from a small, fast animal, hard to catch but delicious when roasted.

That is a pity, said Yukuwa's hands. For we are hungry.

Then you must come home to dinner with me! Yes!

We would be delighted to!

'What are you doing?' Jago said in alarm.

'Eating. Come on.'

You are not from here? the Toala's hands said.

No, away across the sea. I am here as a guest of this Macassan boy's village. They make large boats to catch sea worms which taste terrible.

'Blabbermouth,' said Jago.

They reached a gathering of palm-leaf shelters around two low fires in the shadow of a tall cliff. A few naked children played by throwing sticks and some women wearing loin cloths were cutting the carcass of a small animal.

Your spear is not good in our forest, said the Toala. Too many trees.

Yes, it is hard.

This is better.

The Toala put a dart into the bamboo and blew. The dart hit the carcass the women were working on and the women shouted angrily.

How long have you been here?

We come, we go. But we have been in the forest since the sun was born. Come, come!

The Toala jogged across the clearing and leapt into a tree near the cliff. Yukuwa and Jago climbed after him, but he moved like a monkey, flowing from branch to branch until he was far above the clearing. He steadied a moment and leaped at the cliff, clutching at rock seams, pulling himself to a ledge. He turned to Yukuwa with a welcoming grin.

Yukuwa glanced down at the distant ground, then he was away, not giving himself time to think.

'I think I may stay,' said Jago, clinging to a branch.

Yukuwa turned on the ledge and offered his hand to Jago.

Jago looked at the hand, at the distant ground, at Yukuwa's face. And jumped.

Yukuwa caught him in the air, pulling him to the ledge. 'Wasn't too bad,' he said.

'Shutup.'

The Toala showed them a cave. A cave of ancient art, of many outlined hands.

And Yukuwa felt the hair on his neck rise. 'I know these!'

The Toala nodded. You do these?

People like me, near me, paint hands like this.

Yukuwa placed his hand over an outline and blew. You fill your mouth and blow like this. See? He grinned at Jago.

Jago shrugged.

You have forest like this?

A little bit. We have smaller trees, smaller mountains. Your land is very good. We have seen a waterfall with large butterflies.

The Toala looked sad. We do not go there any more. The Macassans are coming with their houses and rice. We have less forest, animals.

Jago looked uncomfortable.

The Toala people had a feast that night with some quiet chanting songs about their forest and Yukuwa sang about hunting kangaroos.

Next morning the Toala people were gone, taking Yukuwa's spear but leaving a blowpipe and a quiver of darts.

'Maybe we better go home,' Jago said.

22 THE WEDDING

Gali saw them first. He shouted: 'They're back!' ran up to them and crushed them in his arms. 'What happened to you?' he said, and ran off before either of them could say a word.

He came back with Laba and Jago's mother. She cried out as if Jago's dead body was being bounced along the track, and pushed past Laba to get her hands on him. She glared briefly at Yukuwa and dragged Jago into the village, followed by a swirl of Macassans.

Yukuwa stood on the path, alone and hurt.

But Gali stepped out of the rush and smiled at him. 'You were hiding, right? I tell them, but they never listen. And you had nothing to do with the Balanda death, right? Right. I tell them that, too. You have to see Dawu. On the beach. Things have been happening ... Go, go!'

Dawu was floating about in a canoe with Farida. He raced for the shore the moment Yukuwa stepped onto the beach, jumped from the canoe and shook him in the air like a small boy. 'Where've you been?'

Yukuwa told him and showed the blowpipe.

Dawu ignored the blowpipe. 'Then you saw the killing. Saw Madya.'

Farida was nodding, as if some weight had been lifted from her.

'Is he … ?'

'Dead?' Farida said quickly. 'It is over.'

'In the past now,' Dawu said.

'Are the Balandas looking for us?' asked Yukuwa.

'They were. But only in Macassar and they gave up after a day.'

'Gali says something is happening …'

'Oh. Nothing to do with Balandas.' Dawu worked his mangrove foot in the sand. 'Like the canoe? Finished it a moon ago.'

Was it that long? 'It's good. You could sleep in it.'

'But it turns to the right,' said Farida, wrinkling her nose.

Dawu shrugged. 'We'll fix it with the next canoe.'

'When you fix my fence.'

'When you stop criticising.'

And they stopped talking and smiled at each other.

Yukuwa looked curiously at Farida. Madya's wife had been a nervous, bruised woman, but she was gone now. This woman was younger, relaxed, with a smile about her face.

'You are going to make another canoe, then?' Yukuwa said, running his hand along the hull.

'Yes. We have to.'

'There's nothing wrong with this one.'

'But *I* made it. *You* have to learn how to make one yourself before the *Gaddong* sails again. Not that much time.'

'That's all right, you can teach me back home.'

Dawu looked at Yukuwa's face, then turned to Farida. Without a word she waggled her fingers at Yukuwa and walked away.

Yukuwa waited.

Dawu took a quick breath. 'I'm not going home, Yukuwa. Not yet. Not for a long time …'

Yukuwa stopped on the beach, looked at Dawu and waited for the joke. There must be a joke.

'I ... I fit here. I don't have to worry about lugging the mangrove foot from camp to camp, don't have to fall about to throw a spear. The Macassans need my eye, not my foot.'

'But ... what about your people, your totems – *everything*?'

Dawu nodded sadly. 'I have thought of all of that, even of my grave-post, many times.' Then he smiled. 'Life is a long time. I will come home some time. But ...'

Yukuwa waited.

'But now I need you. As my family.'

'As what?'

'I am getting married ...'

Farida caught Yukuwa sitting alone at the edge of the jungle. 'You don't like me, do you?'

'He is one of my fathers. He should come home.'

'I will look after him.'

Yukuwa snapped a twig. The greatest hunter of the Yolngu and he needs a silly woman to feed him. Again.

'I am not Wanduwa.'

Yukuwa turned to Farida in astonishment. *That* close? Is there anything she doesn't know about?

'We talk a lot. You see, Dawu and I are alike. Oh yes, really. We are both strangers in this village. I have lived here all my life but I am still Bugis. It's not so bad – apart from times with Madya – but it is always there. With men it is easier. With Gali they forget he is half-Bugis because he can sing. With Dawu they forget he is Yolngu because he sees fish and because – because he is what he is. But he is still a stranger, like me.'

Farida stretched towards Yukuwa and touched his hand very faintly. 'I need him. I think he needs me.

Please Yukuwa, can I have your father?'

Yukuwa looked down at his hand and felt confused. He wanted to hit her, and he wanted to squeeze her hand. She shouldn't be talking to him like this. She shouldn't.

'You know you can always stay here with us. I'd like that.'

Yukuwa shook his head.

'You want to go home? Of course you do. But you can come back here, can't you? Some time, eh? Give Dawu something to look forward to.'

Yukuwa was kicking pebbles into the water when Jago found him.

'What are you doing?'

'Nothing ...' Dawu was the father who had cut you into manhood, your teacher, the man you saved from the shark. But it didn't matter any more. He was abandoning you, dumping you like a pile of empty shells.

'Never mind. We have to help. Dawu is Taking the Tree. Come on.'

The *Gaddong* had been pulled out of the water at Boatbuilders' Beach for a few new planks and two ribs. Now it would be pulled back into the water.

Yukuwa and Jago joined the crew in pushing the hull of the *Gaddong*, and some villagers hauled ropes. But it wouldn't move.

Then Dawu stepped forward and Took the Tree. He roared at the heaving men, 'Heave now, heave, himbang, himbang!'

And the *Gaddong* moved very slightly.

Dawu rocked his body and made his shouting a song: 'Heave! The Lightning Serpent is chasing you! Demons nibble your toes ...'

The Macassans laughed, and the *Gaddong* shimmied down to the sea.

Yukuwa gave the *Gaddong* a final nudge in the shallows and looked back at Dawu, now with a hand on Gali's shoulder and grinning. He winked at Yukuwa.

Yukuwa hesitated. Dawu has been accepted as a Macassan and he is happy. He is no longer the lonely grouch of Beach of Trees. He has changed, as everything is changing, all the time. Including you.

Yukuwa shrugged, and winked back.

As the wedding drew near, Yukuwa became a messenger.

He took a diamond ring from Jago's mother to Farida on loan. He was warned that if he lost it his head would be fed to the goat.

He carried a red-and-white silk sarong from Dawu to Farida.

A plate of sticky rice, symbolising the cementing of the marriage.

A bowl of hard-boiled eggs cooked in brown sugar syrup and coconut milk, promising a sweet future and the cream of life.

'You must be sick of this,' said Farida.

'No, it's getting to be fun,' said Yukuwa, surprising himself. He was wondering what was next.

Three days before the wedding Gali joined Laba, Jago's mother and Yukuwa for a procession to Farida's house. Laba marched slowly through the village, carrying a small bag of coins on a plate. Jago's wife carried some folded clothing and jewellery. Gali carried special cakes and Yukuwa carried a bowl of bananas, mangos and avocados.

Jago rolled around in the sand, laughing, as Yukuwa passed. Yukuwa flung a small banana at his head without stopping.

On the morning of the wedding Jago stopped giggling enough to help Yukuwa into a black shirt and sarong and kris while his mother raced round the house, looking for a sash.

Yukuwa went outside to join Tale, in white and bearing candles; Laba, with an umbrella to hold over Dawu's head; Gali with his kecapi to play music behind him, and some of the crew to support him.

Dawu stepped out into the sun. He was still a Yolngu hunter, but now he was also a Macassan warrior, with a gold-trimmed blue shirt, a flaring sarong, a rearing turban, a polished kris and a gleaming new foot from Gali.

But Dawu did look not happy. In fact, Yukuwa thought Dawu looked much the same as Ragan did before the circumcision ceremony. Yukuwa immediately began to enjoy himself.

They moved to Farida's house and waited along with the imam, the holy man, of the village mosque, and Jago's mother. Before the house there were bags of rice, brown sugar, nutmegs, cinnamon, leaves and a coconut in a brass mould. Tale added his candles to the clutter.

Eventually Farida descended from her house in her second-best sarong and sat on the coconut. The imam prayed, then the candles were lit and the nutmegs, cinnamon and leaves were added to a china bowl of water. Jago's mother sprinkled water over Farida, then emptied the bowl over her. She went back into her house to bathe and change.

In the afternoon the celebrations began near the village mosque.

Farida arrived, now a princess in flickering gold. She sat beside Dawu in an open canopy of elaborate red carpet with fine white stitching. Before them were two rows of red covers concealing cakes, and many bronze trays, cups and pots of tea. Around these sat a good part of the village, from the Karaeng to Jago.

After a great deal of dancing and beating of drums,

Yukuwa started to sing. He was nervous, but he knew Dawu felt worse.

He sang of the Djang'kawu Sisters after they had created children with their sacred dilly bags. The Sisters had a Brother and when the children grew up the men followed Brother. One day Brother and the men stole the dilly bags while the Sisters were looking for shell fish.

'Typical,' said Jago's mother.

The Sisters tried to get the dilly bags back but the Brother beat his clapping sticks and the men sang with all the power of the dilly bags and drove the Sisters away . . .

'So men have the power,

All the power today . . .' sang Yukuwa.

Farida glowered at him. The crew grinned at Dawu.

But Yukuwa looked at Farida and finished the tale the way Duyga told it:

But Sisters say, 'All right,
Men can look after the power,
We have lost nothing,
We can remember it all!'

Farida laughed, pushed Dawu in the arm and mouthed a silent 'Thank you' to Yukuwa.

After a while Farida quietly left the noisy party and later the Karaeng led Dawu away. They were not seen for three days.

23 THE DEMON ROARS

When the *Gaddong* had gone too far for Yukuwa to shout, he stood at the stern and raised his hand. On the beach Dawu raised his hand and they stayed that way until Dawu had become no more than a fly on the sand.

'You can always come back with us,' Jago said. He looked at Yukuwa and shrugged. 'Come on, help me steer.'

With a new wind blowing from the north east, the *Gaddong* sailed south into fresh waters. It sailed south for three days, loaded with rice, pickled fish, cooking utensils, axes, adzes, tobacco, plates and tea from China, caged cocks, but no canoes. The boat dropped anchor at a sweeping beach on the island of Tanahjampea and a karaeng paddled alongside to negotiate with Laba.

'Marege Beach,' said Jago. 'Called that because most of the boats going to Marege stop here.'

Some wind-blown men paddled other canoes with their outriggers dismantled and placed in the bottom.

'Our canoes are made here. You should stay here to find out how *they* make canoes.'

Yukuwa shook his head without thinking.

'Yeah, I know. You want to go home.'

More than that, Yukuwa thought. You feel like a stone flung into the broad blue sky and just beginning to drop back to its pebbly shore.

Jago turned away. 'All right, you're getting home!'
Yukuwa blinked at Jago's back.
'Who needs you, anyway!' Jago stated.
Oh. 'Hey, you can stay with me!'
Jago stopped.
'Why not?' Yukuwa said. 'The village bores you. Come with us for a season instead. Laba picks you up in the Old People's Camp on the next trip. Easy!'
'Come on,' said Jago flatly. 'We've got to get the canoes aboard.'
The *Gaddong* left Marege Beach next day and sailed south-east to long green islands stretching to the east: Flores slid slowly past, then Adonara, Lambien, Pantar and Alore. A calm stretch between Wetar and Timor, then a stiff breeze carried the *Gaddong* through a scattering of small islands into the open sea.
'The next piece of land you see,' said Laba, 'will be Marege.'
Yukuwa leaned over the sea and could almost smell the pandanus. He stared at the horizon ahead for so long that Jago gave him up for a long conversation with the cocks. When the wind left the *Gaddong* to nod sluggishly in an oily sea, her booms tapping the masts, he wanted to jump into the sea and swim ahead.
Then Gali said, quietly: 'We better take the sails down.'
Yukuwa looked up in hurt astonishment, but Laba was facing the stern and nodding.
Rolling black clouds hissed over a high peak, darkening the water.
'It's going to be bad. All sail down?'
'Yes ... No.' Laba's voice flattened and died. 'Leave them up.'
'All of them?'
Laba pointed. 'All of them. Get the oars out!'
There was a boat off the stern, not much bigger than

the *Gaddong* and with smaller sails sagging on the masts. But it had about twelve long oars out and pulling fast. Like a huge insect scuttling across the water towards the *Gaddong*.

'Pirates ...' said Jago faintly.

'You keep out of the way. Gali, take the boys up to the bow.'

'Wait, wait.' Gali ducked into the cabin and came out with the toy boat he had made.

'You're not serious,' said Tale.

Gali mumbled something and threw the toy boat overboard.

'All right, get up there and load the cannon,' said Laba.

Four oars were thrust from the *Gaddong* and eight of the crew heaved on them. But they were short, made only for moving the boat out of a windless harbour. The *Gaddong* was being rapidly overtaken.

'Sulu pirates,' said Gali, watching the toy boat. 'Ilanun people. They are pirates, like we are trepangers.'

'What does the toy boat do?' Yukuwa asked.

'There are demons and demons. Sometimes they can persuade the pirates that the toy boat is our boat, making them chase it instead of us.'

The pirate boat was not unlike the *Gaddong*. It had the twin rudders, the tripod mast and the wide sails, but at the bow there was a square barrier, hiding and protecting the men behind it.

The pirate boat ran down the toy boat without noticing it.

Tale looked at Gali and shook his head.

'Wrong demons today,' Gali said quietly.

Yukuwa watched the pirate boat until he could hear the beating of drums and the chanting of many men.

'What can we do?' Jago's voice was squeaky. Yukuwa didn't say anything because he could not trust his voice.

'What we *are* doing. Help me with the cannon.'

Laba ordered crewmen to reinforce the long sails by crisscrossing rope between the yards. Tale prayed quickly, then the men pulled out their krises as they lay on the deck, crouched in the cabin and waited.

The pirate boat yawed off its course for a moment and Yukuwa was able to see past the shield and into the boat. There was no deck, just a central plank for the crewmen to work from. Under the plank were the rowers and the fighters.

'There are a hundred of them!' Jago said. He looked at the kris in his hand and the spear in Yukuwa's. He caught the look in Yukuwa's face and his eyes skidded away.

A pirate popped up from behind the barrier, shouting and waving his kris. Gali ignored him and poured fragments of junk iron into the cannon. He wrapped a rag around a stick, poured some oil over it and ignited it with flintstones. The sky behind his head was rolling black.

The pirate boat began to draw level with the *Gaddong*. A sharp report was echoed by a thunderclap. One of the *Gaddong*'s oarsmen jumped his hand from the sudden scar on his oar and looked at his mate in alarm. Laba shouted and all the oarsmen pulled in their oars and flattened themselves on the deck.

A pirate leapt to the side of his boat and shouted in anger. Laba stood up with his pistol and pointed it at the pirate. He fired and the pirate fell back onto the rowers. Another pirate stepped out from the barrier and hurled a grapnel at the bow of the *Gaddong*. The grapnel clutched at the anchor and the pirate heaved on the attached rope. Jago leapt at the grapnel and hacked at the rope with his kris. There were five men on the rope and the pirate boat was nosing closer.

Jago shouted in triumph as the rope parted and the men

tumbled backwards, but there were many grapnels in the air, clutching at the *Gaddong*'s side, cabin, tiller, masts. The oars were pulled out of the water as the boats were drawn towards each other. The men on both boats were roaring at each other, the sound battering Yukuwa's ears.

Gali swivelled the cannon towards the open pirate boat and lifted the firestick. But the pirate boat emptied onto the *Gaddong*, a great wave of men jumping across the water, men with teeth clamped on krises, men waving krises, men shrieking.

A man landed on the cannon, swinging at Gali. Gali brought the firestick from the touch-hole to stop the thrust, then he was driven back. Yukuwa heard Jago shouting, 'Throw,' as if from a great distance, and threw the spear, without a target and without knowing where it went.

A pirate with a sliced nose lunged and Yukuwa hurled himself back, beyond the sweep of his blade. His hand thumped against a rope, clutched and he swung out over the water. He swung back to drive his feet into the back of the pirate, then he was gone.

Jago was reaching for the firestick on the deck. He picked it up, stepped across to the cannon ...

And the sliced-nose pirate was leaping at him.

'Jago!'

Jago looked up at Yukuwa in surprise, shifted his eyes and lifted his kris, but too late, too late. The man's foot landed on the deck, his kris swung forward and he kept running towards the cabin. Jago dropped his kris, clutched at his side and flopped on the deck.

Yukuwa knelt beside Jago, trying to help. Another pirate ran over him, sprawling him over the firestick.

'Get out!' He shrieked and lashed about him with the firestick.

He looked up from Jago and everything he saw was tinged with red: the dark line on the water, Laba leaning into a long thrust, Tale swinging on the yard to kick at heads, the crew heaving, giving way, more pirates in the air between the pirate boat and the *Gaddong*. And the cannon, the iron barrel of Balanda demons, pointing at them.

Yukuwa looked at the firestick in his hand and remembered the soldier with the cannon in the Rotterdam Fort. Just a touch of fire …

He touched the base of the cannon with the firestick. The cannon bucked …

The roar shuddered into his bones. Then a terrible shriek, as if a thousand demons were clawing into the air. Smoke hung before the cannon for a moment, before it was snatched aside. Men sprawled over the pirate boat, holding themselves together, a man without a face …

The dark line on the water passed over the boats. The wind howled through the ropes, filling the *Gaddong*'s sails, pushing them hard against the network of ropes, making the masts creak and splinter. The *Gaddong* dragged the pirate boat sideways, scooping up the sea, then the grapnel ropes began to snap. Pirates stopped fighting and leaped back onto their boat, or jumped, or fell into the sea. With a last ripple of snapping rope the *Gaddong* broke free and fled with the wind.

24 LAST VOYAGE

The long sails blew themselves to pieces despite the reinforcing ropes. The remaining sail, the jib, was rolled and ragged but it still caught the wind and the *Gaddong* foamed across the dark sea for nine hours. For much of that time Yukuwa and Gali worked on Jago's wound.

When the wind dropped, Tale held ceremonies for the men who had died, and their bodies were slid into the sea.

'Five gone,' Laba said heavily. 'Five friends. We had nothing for them – rice, tobacco, pieces of iron, we had nothing . I should have let them have what they wanted.'

'No,' said Tale.

Laba looked around, at the crewmen in their bloodied bandages, the men drooping over the matting deck, the two men still unconscious and his son lying pale in his cabin. 'No?'

'They didn't want what we carry. They wanted us.'

Laba nodded. 'For the slave market. It is over now. Look at us, do we turn around and go home?'

'Marege ...' Jago was trying to shout from the cabin, but it was little more than a whisper.

'Yes, yes, we're Macassans.' Laba smiled a little. 'Let's see if we can get a sail up.'

By the next day the *Gaddong* sailed under the patched jib and bare yards. The second day the fragments of the long sails and some of the matting deck had been combined for a mainsail and the boat was creaming across the sea. In the afternoon one of the unconscious seamen woke up. But during the night Jago called for Yukuwa.

Yukuwa knelt beside Jago. 'Is there something wrong?'

'Not me. It's him. I think he's stopped breathing.' Jago nodded at the remaining unconscious seaman.

Yukuwa held the back of his hand over the seaman's mouth and watched for any movement in the soft hairs of the hand. He left the cabin to wake Laba on deck. The body was taken out of the cabin and released into the sea at dawn.

'That was so gentle,' said Jago. 'One time he was breathing, then one time he was not breathing. Wonder if Mustari went like that.'

'Hey, stop that.'

'Stop what? I think I will go back to sleep.'

For the rest of the night Yukuwa sat beside Jago, listening to his breathing.

Jago awoke to the smell of Tale's rice and fish and he ate as if he was trying to make up for the meals he had missed.

'Hey, that was a great fight,' Jago said through his rice.

'It was terrible.' Yukuwa shook his head.

'But we won!'

'Six died.'

'But we won. We fired the cannon at them. Gali fired the cannon, no, no, he lost the firestick. Threw it to me. *I* must have fired the cannon.'

Yukuwa rammed rice into his mouth.

'I can remember. I killed a man with my kris. Then I got to the cannon ... I didn't, did I? You? It was you?'

'Every time I close my eyes it comes back. It won't let go.'

'But we won. And Mustari missed it.'

Yukuwa watched Jago shuffling along the deck like an old man. But the boy was coming back.

'Can't you see any fish at all?' Jago said.

'No.'

'Dawu could. Any time.'

'I'm not Dawu.'

'We should throw you overboard.' And he grinned.

A couple of days later, Jago pointed his kris at a flat green line on the horizon and almost danced. 'Marege! You're home, almost home. You can wrestle with crocodiles again.'

'Stop waving the kris about. You got to keep quiet.'

'Ah, Tale is going to take the stitches out any time.' Jabbing, slicing the air.

'Put it away.'

'You're an old woman. I could kill a crocodile like this. Ah ...' Jago held his arm high, the kris shining in the sun. His face was suddenly bloodless.

'What's wrong?'

'Nothing. I'm going to sit down.'

Next day, Jago was leaning back in the cabin.

'Jago, about that crocodile ...'

'Bragging again.'

'No. Jago, you saw it wrong. I didn't hit it.'

'I saw the spear.'

'It was Ragan. I'm sorry.'

Jago laughed. 'It doesn't matter.'

'To me it does.'

'All right. But to me it doesn't.'

Two days later Jago was lying flat with a face like dried grass.

'Maybe I should stay in Marege with you, after all,' Jago said.

'Good, you'll like it. No cannon.'

'Just for a season. Laba won't mind.'

'We'll have mud crabs on the beach. I'll show you how to spear fish.'

'If you can see any.'

'Ah, you will see them by yourself. You'll be better with a spear than me. You'll have to be.'

'I've got a good eye. Always had one.'

'You going to try to eat the rice now? Just a little bit.'

'Can't now. Belly is very heavy.'

A day later.

'It was good in Celebes, eh?'

'Most of it.'

'When we took our money to the Balanda sweet shop. We were kings!'

'For a day. Better was the fishing in the butterfly pool?'

'Nuh. Was better when that monkey got you with a nut.'

'What about you and Hals? First time you just wanted to run away.'

'Wonder how Madya felt.'

'Felt when?'

'When they hanged him. When he died.'

'Oh ...'

'Forget it. It's been good, very good. All of it.'

Jago looked unsteadily at his father as the shadow of a frown crept across his face. 'Where's Mustari?' he whispered.

Then he moved his eyes to Yukuwa, seemed to think for a bit, and moved his lips briefly.

Part Four

25 SONGMAN

Yukuwa walked alone to the oyster cliffs and sat on the sand.

It was over now. He had stepped onto Old People's Camp and been crushed by Duyga for a long time. Wapiti and the Widow had stroked him as if uncertain he was really there, but Gathul had greeted him with a simple thump on the shoulder. He was back.

But he had stood between Gali and Laba on the spit, as the boy was washed many times and dressed in white and carried to his grave on a board. Then he had stepped from Tale's soft song and the rippling Macassan flags to the quiet dance of the Yolngu people, echoing the sadness and marking the boy's passage among them.

The Macassan feasts that followed, mixing grief with joy, had come and gone.

Now he simply wanted to be alone with a memory of Jago, to somehow work it all out.

Later, Ragan came to the oyster cliffs and sat beside Yukuwa.

'You're crying, wawa,' he said.

Yukuwa smeared his eyes with the back of his arm. 'It's the place.'

'Oh ...' Ragan looked about him, at the oyster cliffs and the ragged *Gaddong*.

'Not now. Before. When we were here, making a song, and he came here to tell us about Dawu's foot ...'

'So long ago. He didn't like being called your wawa, your brother.'

'Out there Tale was saying the names of God for him, stroking his big finger to make an easier passage for his spirit. He opened his eyes and said hello to Laba, he wanted to see a friend he had lost. Then he saw me, but his voice had gone.'

Ragan looked at the sand and waited.

'With his lips he said, "Hello wawa." He closed his eyes, sighed and the shape of his face changed slightly.'

Ragan was silent for a while. Then he took Yukuwa by the arm and led him along the beach.

'We going hunting now?'

'Not now.'

Ragan led him before the shelters and picked up his didgeridoo. Bawi and Gathul wandered down to him.

Ragan sat him down and passed him the clapping sticks. 'You have a song to sing,' he said.

Yukuwa looked at the sticks and shook his head. 'I can't,' he said.

But Gathul squatted in the sand, then his mothers, his other fathers, his brothers, his sisters, his mother-in-law ...

'I can't,' he said, as his clapping sticks clicked idly in his hands.

You're not a songman. You're not a hunter, you're nothing. Like Madya, what'd he say? He was a 'worm collector'. You're not even that. Except ...

The sticks rippled.

Except he wasn't. He was a Fighting Cock of Macassar, because his great grandfather got into a huge battle, and everyone knows about the battle because people – like Gali – sing about battles. There should be a song about the *Gaddong*'s battle. No. There should be a song about the warrior Jago.

The sticks beat a rhythm.

And a song about the wedding of Dawu, and Gali's kris fight, and Hals, and the ghost people. You *can* sing a tale, you've learned how from Bawi's gossip songs, Duyga's Dreamtime songs, Gali's boat songs. You've practised on the *Gaddong* and at Dawu's wedding.

Ragan played the didgeridoo beside him.

You've got a song to sing. You've seen caged men, heard a cannon roar, smelled Macassar. And lost a friend. You can sing of laughter, anger, terror and, sometimes, of the soft pain Jago has left.

Yukuwa sighed. He wasn't a good hunter, never would be a warrior, but he could try to be a songman. As long as people wanted to listen.

He began to sing.

Nhina warraw' ŋura,
ŋaku warryun malwarra
Nhama djambatjŋu
Mirrinyu.
Mayan namba
Wuŋuli

Sitting down in the shade
Pulling the canoe into the water
Looking for dugong
Clouds standing in the sea
The shadow stays with them.

AFTERWORD

Fifty-six years later, in 1776, Lieutenant James Cook sailed up the east coast of Australia, passing north of the Old People's Camp and into Macassan water.

In 1788 Governor Phillip started an English convict colony in Port Jackson, called Sydney Town.

In 1803 Lieutenant Matthew Flinders encountered six Macassan praus within sight of Nhulunbuy.

In 1876 there were seventeen Aborigines living in Macassar.

In 1884 the South Australian government, controlling the Northern Territory, demanded that Macassans buy licences for trepanging. Macassans soon ceased to sail to Marege, leaving much of their language and culture with the Aborigines they had dealt with. The Aborigines made many dug-out canoes when the Macassans ceased to come.

In 1944 the Dutch were evicted from the East Indies as Indonesia became an independent state. Celebes became Sulawesi and Macassar became Ujung Pandang, the name of the fort that the Dutch called Fort Rotterdam.

The Toala people have disappeared.

The Old People's Camp is now Macassar Beach.

The coastal Aborigines of the Northern Territory call all white people 'balandas'.

About the author

Allan Baillie was born in Scotland in 1943, but has lived in Australia since he was seven years old. On leaving school he worked as a journalist and travelled extensively. He is the author of many highly acclaimed novels for children, and a prize-winning picture book:

Adrift (Shortlisted for the 1985 Australian Children's Book of the Year Award, and winner of the 1983 Kathleen Fidler Award)
Little Brother (Highly commended in the 1986 Australian Children's Book of the Year Awards and shortlisted for the 1986 Guardian Children's Fiction Award)
Riverman (Winner of the 1988 IBBY Honour Diploma [Australia], shortlisted for the 1987 Guardian Children's Fiction Award and shortlisted for the 1987 Australian Children's Book of the Year Award)
Eagle Island
Megan's Star (Shortlisted for the 1989 Australian Children's Book of the Year Award)
Hero (A Children's Book Council of Australia Notable Book 1991)
The China Coin (Shortlisted for the 1992 Guardian Children's Fiction Award and the 1992 Adelaide Festival Literary Award, and winner of the 1992 Australian

Multicultural Children's Literature Award)
Magician
Drac and the Gremlin (Winner of the 1989 Australian Picture Book of the Year Award).

Allan now lives in Sydney with his wife and two children and writes full time.